THE PROMISED LAND DIARIES

1

Persia's Brightest Star

The Diary of Queen Esther's Attendant

Persian Empire

470s B.C.

Diary One
Coming to King Xerxes' Palace

479 B.C.

The Servants' Quarters, My New Home

It's early in the morning, hours before sunrise, and I'm already awake. All night I listened to the horrible howls of the jackals. First there was one, and then there was another. Now a whole pack is lifting their noses to the moon and moaning.

They're very unsettling, but the lynx are even worse. They stalk the palace walls just beyond the courtyard and try to hunt the peacocks roosting in the orange trees. They can't reach them, but they create terrible havoc. The birds cry a pitiful wail, which sounds just like a hurt child. Then they scamper fearfully through the trees. The golden cats snarl and leap against the brick walls again and again.

I know I'm safe, but how I wish I were nearer to Mother and Father. Their quarters are in another wing of the palace. I could go to them, but the long halls are dark at night, and spooky too.

Instead, I've lit a candle. It sits in a cubbyhole in the wall near my bed. The flame glows yellow while silvery moonbeams slip through my window. They shed just enough light to write to my dear friend, you, my little diary! You will comfort me, won't you?

It's a strange time in the palace right now. Queen Vashti has left. Or perhaps I should say King Xerxes has removed her from the throne and from her position as his wife. Tomorrow I was to become one of her personal attendants. At twelve years old, I'm the youngest ever chosen from the palace maids! Mother said I should be very proud. I am!

That explains why I live in the northern quarters of the palace and Mother and Father live in the servants' wing farther south. Father is the master gardener, and mother is a kettle stirrer. They must live closer to the gardens and kitchen. My quarters are near the harem, the throne room, and the great halls.

It was planned that I would live here while I was an attendant in training. If I did well and Queen Vashti approved of me, I would move to the royal harem, where she lived in a separate wing.

I feel pleased as I look around my new apartment. It's nicer than the one I used to have. There's a large wooden chest filled with lots of new clothes—shirts, trousers, caftans, and head scarves. They're more colorful and made of finer materials now. New rugs cover the bare stone floor. There's only one problem—I don't know how long I'll stay now that the queen has left.

Mother tucked me into bed last night, and she told me an interesting rumor. "Susiana," she said as she gently pushed the blankets under my chin, "we hear that King Xerxes is looking for a new wife."

The "we" she mentioned is the servants. They're the eyes and ears of the palace. News travels like lightening among them. It's not uncommon for their silent feet to prowl the hallways and glean information that the queen, or even the king, doesn't know yet.

"A new wife?" I was surprised. "Already, Mother?"

She nodded her head.

"Where?" I asked her. "Where is he looking for this new wife?"

"Everywhere," she told me. "It seems that soon, maybe even as soon as tomorrow, the most beautiful girls in the kingdom will be brought to the palace. They will receive their beauty treatments and will be readied to meet the king. The one who pleases the king most will become our new queen."

The jackals are quiet now. They've slipped into the night and disappeared into their dens near the mountains. I spot pale patches of orange and pink sky through my window near the roof. Morning has arrived, dear friend, and I'm very sleepy! Perhaps I can rest for just a little while.

Later

I was awakened again this morning, this time to a great commotion outside of my door. I heard leather booties shuffle up and down the hallway, muffled voices, the creak of a door, my door, opening then closing.

"Susiana?" a familiar voice called to me. I pulled the covers over my head and moaned.

"It's me—Roxana." Roxana is another of the maids. She's my best friend. She's thirteen years old.

"Do you know what has taken place?" she asked me. I had no choice. I had to get up. I was trying to dress quickly, but it wasn't an easy process. I slipped on a fresh pair of blue trousers and tugged at the drawstring. I was astonished at their softness. The ones I used to wear were cotton. These felt more like silk.

I said, "Find me a shirt, will you?" Roxana rummaged through my chest and pulled one out. I slipped it over my head, and it fell to my knees. It had a round neck with a vertical slit. I quickly pulled the four small buttons through their loops.

"Do you know what has happened?" she repeated, this time with more excitement.

"I don't know if I know," I told her, "but I have a feeling that you've come to tell me.

You'll have to wait a moment. I can't have a proper conversation until I'm fully dressed."

I found a matching yellow caftan and pulled it over my head. It was the first time I'd worn this one, and I ran my hands over the smooth fabric. It felt soft, silky, like the trousers. The hem fell to my feet.

Dressing was quite an elaborate ritual. I always had to check to make sure I had everything on just right. I didn't want to be scolded today. "Trousers, shirt, caftan . . . ," I mumbled under my breath. Something was missing. "Roxana! What am I missing?"

She laughed at me. "Your head scarf! But your hair is a mess. Come here. I'll fix it for you." I gave her my brush, and we sat on the bed together. She ran the brush gently through my tangled hair. "All right. Can I talk to you now?" she asked.

"Yes, talk to me now. What's so urgent?" I smiled to myself, but she couldn't see my face. I was sure she was going to tell me that the girls had arrived in the royal harem.

"Guess who arrived this morning?" she whispered in a conspiratorial fashion.

I knew it! I swung around and faced her. "Would it be the most beautiful girls in the kingdom, by any chance?"

Her shoulders dropped in disappointment. "I should've known you'd know. You know everything. Who told you this time? Damaris?"

Damaris is a very large servant who has an equally large mouth. She couldn't keep a secret if her life depended upon it. "No. It was Mother, and I don't know who told her. Have you seen them?"

"Of course not. No one's seen them. They were brought in through the carriage gate and quickly ushered into the harem. Apparently, Hegai guards them fiercely."

Hegai is the king's eunuch, and he's in charge of the new girls in the harem. Only a few chosen servants and the king have ever seen the harem, but spectacular rumors about it swirl through the palace. Everyone knows that the girls are kept in the harem just to please the king. They're taught to play musical instruments, dance, and sing.

Many times the servants stay up late into the evening, telling stories about them. We gather in one of the girls' apartments and sit around a corsi. This short wooden table is made in such a way that we can light a fire in a container beneath it. It keeps us warm on bitterly cold Persian evenings. Sometimes we even eat and sleep near it.

One night we gathered together with bowls of nuts and fruit between us. "I've heard that the girls in the harem wear diamond earrings as large as walnuts!" said one of the girls.

Roxana rolled her eyes. "Yes, well, I've heard they wear ropes of white and black pearls that drape to the floor. When they walk, a servant has to dash behind them and carry the pearls just like the train of a dress is carried!"

"I wouldn't mind that job!" another of the girls said. We all laughed uncontrollably.

"That's nothing," said Ava. "Did you hear about the story of the harem ghost?"

We gasped.

"I didn't think so," she said and smiled. "Not long ago, the most beautiful girl in the harem was in the bathhouse late at night. She was the king's favorite, and all of the other girls were very jealous of her. She'd just finished her bath when she noticed that she was all alone. All she could hear was the drip, drip, drip of the water as it fell from the pipe in the cold, stone wall. She called for her eunuch, but her voice just echoed back to her—a hollow, lonely call. "

Ava paused to make sure she had our attention. She leaned closer for effect. "Later that night, the king sent the eunuch to bring her to him. The eunuch searched for her everywhere, but he couldn't find her. Finally, in desperation, he went to the bathhouse. There she was, floating in the water, dead."

We all sat and stared at one another. "What about the ghost?" I finally managed to ask. "You said there was a harem ghost."

Ava held up her hand. "I'll get to that," she said and cleared her throat.

"Well," she continued, "it's said that late at night, a beautiful ghost with long, silken black hair, who looks exactly like the maiden, floats through the halls of the harem. She cries out for her eunuch—the one who never saved her."

I was pretty sure Ava had made this up, but I had to admit it was a pretty good story.

I stood in front of the mirror and adjusted my hair braid, then my head scarf. I felt nervous for some reason.

"Susiana, I have something else to tell you." Roxana's voice was lower now, and she looked serious. "There's another rumor. I don't know if you've heard it or not."

I looked at her and shook my head.

"Since you were already chosen to be one of Queen Vashti's attendants," she said, "I've heard that you may be needed right away to attend these girls in the harem."

I sat back down on the bed. Why did I feel suddenly nervous? All I could think of was that harem ghost. "Are you sure you heard right?" I asked. She nodded.

I had to talk to Mother and Father. "Roxana, I have to go. I'll find you in a while." I sped out of the room and ran down the hallway. I stopped long enough to gather up the bottom of my caftan so I wouldn't trip.

In the Palace Garden

I love this place, and I knew I would find Father here. Sure enough, he was in the garden on the east side of the palace terrace. Damaris made sure I knew this when I passed her in the hall. Everyone knows she eavesdrops. It's pointless to ask things like how she knew I was looking for Father. "Thank you, Damaris," I said with a smile. "You're quite helpful at times."

I heard her snort as I turned away, and I laughed. Father had a huge smile on his face when he saw me. "Welcome to paradise, Susi!" he sang out. The gardens are called paradise because they are so beautiful. They are edged with elegant cypress trees and dotted with groves of fruit and nut trees like orange, lemon, peach, walnut, almond, and pistachio.

I walked down the marble pathway and saw the tail of a peacock as it disappeared into the trees. Two turtledoves balanced on a branch above my head. It was easy to think this was heaven on earth.

Long ago Father had taught me the names of all of the flowers and plants here. I passed yellow jonquils, white narcissus, and purple hyacinths. Little ruby roses climbed the walls beside the bushes of oleander. On the right I spotted the tulips. They're my favorite. On the left were rows of saffron crocus. Three long, red-orange stigmas peeked out of each flower. These threads are dried and then crumbled or powdered to season and color food. I took a deep breath. The air was heavily perfumed with all these flowers.

Father was seated near a splashing fountain. He was giving instructions to one of his many workers.

I'm very proud of him. He's responsible for the many palace gardens, and they're very important to the king. The flowers are grown not just to beautify the gardens and courtyards, but to supply the feasts and banquets held in the palace. Hundreds of his flowers are picked and used to decorate the tables and windowsills.

There is a separate flower garden used primarily for that purpose, as well as a separate fruit orchard, vineyard, and huge vegetable garden. Father's fruits, nuts, and vegetables are used to prepare the meals every day.

I wrapped my arms around him and sat close. "Father," I said, "I'm scared."

He looked at me, concerned. "Why, Susi? Has something happened?"

"There's a rumor that I'll be chosen to attend the harem," I told him. "Did you know that girls from all over the kingdom have just arrived?"

He nodded.

"I don't know why I'm so nervous," I said. "I suppose it's because everything about the royal harem is so mysterious." I was thinking about the ghost, but I felt silly mentioning it to him. "I liked Queen Vashti, but I don't know about Hegai, Father. I've heard that he can be—"

"Susi, hush," Father interrupted.

He put a gentle finger over my lips. "God prepares all of us for our places in life. If you are chosen, then you are already equipped to do the job. Don't worry."

He reached into the folds of his robe and pulled out an orange and several walnuts. Then he cracked the hard shells against the side of the fountain and picked out the nutmeat for me. It was time for him to return to work, and I watched his back as he moved away. I ate the walnuts, then peeled the rind from the orange and ate that too. It was sweet and soft, and the juice dripped down my chin.

I wished I could stay in the garden forever. It's so quiet and peaceful and safe. I watched the water in the fountain as it spilled from one tier to the next. An uneasy feeling has settled on me—not a bad feeling, just an uneasy one. Like the feeling you get when you know something important is just around the corner but you don't know what. After sitting here a while, with you, my little diary, I feel ready to go back inside. I will tuck you in my pocket now . . .

Later

I found Mother in one of the kitchens. It was quite a change from Father's quiet, peaceful paradise. A special lunch was being prepared for a group of the king's noblemen. Servants were running here and there, shouting orders. Mother was frantic.

"Susi!" she cried when she saw me. "The Lord is faithful! He has brought me an extra set of hands." She stuck a long wooden spoon in my face and motioned with her head toward the copper kettle beside her. "The wretched pudding maker is ill today, and I have her job as well as my own," she said. "Please stir."

I watched the activity as I moved my spoon through the bubbling wheat pudding. I was always fascinated by the workings of the palace kitchen. There were at least twenty brass brewing pots—the cooks call them braziers—heating up. Some were used to roast the meat of the kebabs until it was brown and dripping with juice. Big coffee jugs were placed over the coals of others. Coffee brewed on a brazier is very frothy and tasty, and it's a welcome treat after a meal.

Mother moved from one kettle to another, stirring. There was soup to start. I love this soup. It is thick, made with wheat, spinach, peas, and lentils. The main dishes—quince stew and lamb kebabs—would be served second. Side dishes, like caviar, eggplant, and wheat pudding, are set out too.

Then, when the guests think they can't eat another bite, the most luscious sweets are served. Sherbets are very popular because they are cold and refreshing on Persia's hot summer days. The most common flavors are orange, lemon, pomegranate, rosewater, and quince.

I noticed that the *baklava* was already prepared and on the table. Oh, how my mouth watered for a taste. It's wonderful, made with almonds, sugar, egg yolks, and a few other things I can't remember.

The servants are allowed to eat what's left, and there's usually a lot left over. It's better to make more and allow the guests to eat until they are full. It would be a disgrace to run out of food in any household, mother always told me, but in the palace of the king, it would be a disaster.

Thank goodness for these special feasts. Most of the time the servants eat bread and barley cakes washed down with wine or beer. Boiled meat isn't even very common. I'm lucky to have Mother and Father in the kitchen and the garden. We usually eat the most scrumptious foods.

I'm Going to the Harem!

This morning I learned that Roxana was right as usual. I was summoned to serve in the royal harem. Just after sunrise there was a loud rap on my door. One of the royal eunuchs stood there.

It wasn't Hegai—he's too important to bother with someone like me. It was another eunuch by the name of Biztha.

His skin was a beautiful chocolate brown and he wore a long tunic the color of a green sea. He wore a shorter tan tunic over the first. It was edged in the brown color of his skin. It was worn open, and I could see an orange sash tied just above his waist. A long, gauzy scarf was wrapped, turban style, around his head.

"The king requests your service in the royal harem," he announced in a deep, monotone voice. "It is a privilege and an honor to serve His Royal Highness, King Xerxes the Great."

He waited outside the door while I dressed. Then he led the way to this private part of the palace. We stepped through enormous wooden doors into a labyrinth of dimly lit halls and passageways. I could feel my heart thumping in my chest. The lull of soft voices and the whine of the stringed dulcimer echoed off the stone walls and bare floors.

I followed Biztha down one of the passageways and through another set of wide, heavy doors. We stepped into a huge room, and it took a moment for my eyes to adjust. The room was thick with a mist that hung in the air. The smoky vapor swirled from brass burners, and I realized it was incense. It had an unusual scent. It wasn't unpleasant, but woodsy and slightly musky.

Biztha introduced me to Sohelia, an older, experienced attendant, and told me she would teach me my duties and educate me about the customs of the harem. I didn't really know what to expect in this mysterious and exotic place, but I tried not to fear the worst. It's completely different from my own world.

Sohelia seemed nice enough. She seemed wise and patient too. She told me about the incense and how it's used to soften and purify the skin and hair. It's also burned at night to help the girls sleep peacefully and to give them sweet dreams.

She took me on a brief tour of the huge harem. One of the corridors, she pointed out, led to the bathhouse. I again thought of the beautiful girl in Ava's story, and I shuddered. Another corridor led to the harem courtyard, and another led to the infirmary where the girls go when they're ill. We passed a laundry, a storeroom, a kitchen, a food corridor, a fruit room, a library, and a mosque. There was a separate corridor for the rooms where the eunuchs sleep and a separate bathhouse for them as well.

I feared I'd never learn my way around this place. I'd get lost, no one would ever find me, and someday a girl like Ava would tell the story of a maid who disappeared in the harem. I must have sighed deeply and looked disturbed, because Sohelia cupped my face with her hand and smiled. "Don't worry," she said. "You'll learn it all in time. You haven't even been here two hours."

I followed her into another huge room, which I learned was the inner courtyard. A fountain splashed into a large marbled pool. Platforms were piled high with luxurious pillows and cushions. These, I noticed, were upholstered with gold and silver thread. Thick

Persian rugs covered the floor. Where there were no rugs, there was marble or intricate tile.

The little gazelles that loped about the room made me laugh. They pranced in and out of the courtyard at their choosing. Gold birdcages reached from floor to ceiling. I couldn't resist, and left Sohelia for a moment to satisfy my own curiosity. There were parrots, macaws, doves, canaries, nightingales, and exotic varieties I couldn't name.

The ceilings were a canvas of ornate paintings and more tile. Windows were latticed or made of jeweled Persian glass. They looked out to the courtyard or to the mountains in the distance. The sun shimmered through the intricate latticework and bathed the room in gold.

Sohelia explained that there was enough window for the girls to peek out and see the world beyond but not enough that the girls could be seen from the outside. Once a girl entered the harem, she spent most of her days and nights there. If she was fortunate enough to be allowed out of the palace, she was carefully guarded. If she was allowed to leave the covered carriage in which she rode, she was required to wear her veil, which completely covered her face. Only her eyes were exposed.

"You'll see the girls tomorrow," Sohelia told me. "They're all very beautiful, but there's one who is exquisite beyond measure. Tell me if you can find the one of whom I speak."

When I returned to my apartment this evening, everything seemed very stark and drab by comparison. I'm sure that I will feel very drab as well after I see the girls!

I've Seen the Beauty Treatments . . .

I entered the harem today just after sunrise. Sohelia sleeps in the servants' quarters, which are in one of the dark passageways. That's where most of the harem attendants live. So far I have been allowed to keep my little apartment. I hope it stays that way, but I'm quite sure it won't. Most of the attendants of the harem don't mix with the rest of the palace servants. It's all very secretive.

The harem bustled with activity this morning. There are so many girls I can't possibly count them. It's strange to think that one of them will become our future queen. I studied them very closely because of what Sohelia said to me yesterday. One is exquisite, she said. Who is it? I keep searching.

As the girls began their beauty regime today, each of us, the attendants, worked on four or five at a time. I assisted Sohelia, because I'm still in training. It's just the start of a year's worth of treatments intended not only to beautify the girls' bodies but also to cleanse and purify them. A girl can't be presented to the king until she's completely purified.

Sohelia didn't waste any time. She handed me a bowl of hens' eggs and told me to separate the whites from the yokes. She whipped the egg whites with a deft hand, stuck a squirrel-tail brush in the bowl, and applied the mixture to the corners of the girls' eyes. Then in one swift movement, she dumped the thick, golden yolks onto their heads and massaged the goop into their hair. She covered their heads with pieces of muslin.

My eyes were wide as I watched this process. I'd never done anything but eat eggs. I had no idea they were so useful. "The whites will soften the fine lines around their eyes, and the yolks will moisturize their hair," Sohelia told me. She reached over and rubbed my braid between her fingers. "You could use a few beauty treatments yourself, Susiana," she added.

There were a lot of giggles during these beauty treatments. I have to admit most of these girls looked rather silly and not at all like future queens!

I Think I've Spotted Her!

I'm quite sure I know the identity of the exquisite beauty Sohelia mentioned to me on my first day. She's a girl by the name of Esther—by far the most beautiful of all the girls, but there's something else about her. She has an unusual presence. She's remarkably kind and humble and sweet, and that is part of her beauty.

Some of the girls here are rude and mean spirited, and I don't like them at all. I'm reminded continuously of the story Ava told. Just like in the story, I sense the jealousy among them. Every one of these girls knows why she's here; they all want to be queen more than anything in the world. Only one will be chosen, so they all compete with one another.

Everyone, that is, except Esther.

The beautiful Esther seems detached from most of the activities and most of the other girls here. To pass the time, the girls tell riddles or play simple games. Yet Esther usually sits by herself. She occupies her time with a book or with a pen and paper. I suspect she keeps a diary like I do.

Just the other day, a girl by the name of Moj pushed another girl by the pool. It was very slippery, so the girl fell and broke her foot and landed in the infirmary. Of course Moj denied it, but I saw it, and a lot of the other girls did too. The girls have already made names for themselves. Moj is definitely trouble and one to watch out for.

I've Learned a Secret

Roxana found me in the hall on the way to my apartment tonight. We whispered in the shadows. "Guess what I heard?" she said.

"What?" I asked her.

She got very close to my ear. "Esther is a Jew!"

I just looked at her. "Roxana, I knew there was something different about her!"

She nodded her head.

Roxana and I are Jewish too. There are a few of us in the palace but not many. Roxana was born within these walls, but Mother and Father came to work here when I was a baby. It was then that my name was changed to Susiana. It's a Persian name that means "lily." It's a common practice to be given a Persian name if you're not Persian. It's usually one that suits your character or qualities.

"Well, we know that Esther isn't a Jewish name, Roxana," I said low.

"It's not. Her real name is Hadassah," she said. "Esther means 'star' in Persian."

I was confused. Why was a Jewish girl brought into the Persian harem now? Those girls were being groomed to become queen. Esther could never become queen of the Persian Empire. Or could she? Suddenly we heard a shuffle in the hallway. Roxana pulled me deeper into a dark corner. "Roxana, how do you know all of this? Who else knows?"

"I overheard Father talking to Mother. He knows Mordecai, Esther's cousin. He's an official in the palace. We're the only ones who know." She put her hand over my mouth. "Susiana," she said in a low voice, "you can't tell a soul. Who knows what could happen to Esther if someone found out."

I heard the shuffle again. Someone was listening. I was sure of it. "Go to bed," she said urgently. "But remember what I said." She put a finger over my mouth. "Not a word."

I'm Moving

Hegai was so impressed with Esther that he decided to move her into a special part of the harem. She was given seven maids of her very own. Sohelia is one and I am another. Sohelia must have put in a good word for me. Why else would I be chosen?

I thought back to Father's words in the garden—"God prepares all of us for our places in life. If you are chosen, then you are already equipped to do the job." I miss Mother and Father. It's been several days since I've seen them. I hope it won't be harder for me to spend time with them now that I'll be in the harem.

I Never Knew Beauty Had a Sound . . .

But so much beauty is here. The most beautiful girls live in the harem, and our surroundings are layers of beauty.

In fact, beauty surrounds beauty: Tiger skins are draped over the divans. Red velvet curtains separate one part of the room from another.

Large gilded mirrors hang on the walls. Enormous pots with towering palms and ferns sit in each corner. Splashing fountains rise up out of the marble floor like sea serpents. It's almost as if you can taste and feel and hear the beauty.

I spend all my time with Esther now. She's very gracious to me, and she seems embarrassed by all the attention.

Sohelia gave me a beautiful fan made of peacock feathers. It's my job, she told me, to stand behind Esther and gently wave the feathers to cool her. When Esther saw me, she immediately jumped up. "Oh no, Susiana, you don't have to do that for me. I can do that myself." A crimson blush crept across her usually pale face.

I told her it was my job and that it was a pleasure for me. Still, she asked if she might have the fan. She waved the feathers to cool both of us. Sohelia frowned when she saw Esther, but there was nothing either of us could do. She insisted.

A cage of nightingales entrances Esther, and

she usually stays close to them. I sat beside her one day, and we watched the small birds frolic together. "Aren't they exquisite, Susiana?" she asked me. I looked at them more closely. They were pretty birds, but certainly not extraordinary. They're a plain russet brown, but I suppose they do have sweet faces.

"Esther," I said, "there are more beautiful birds than these. What about the parrots? What about the macaws? Their colors are amazing."

"It's not their colors, Susiana," she said. "Anyone can wear beautiful clothes. It's their nature. They sing to me with such sweet sadness late into the night. They sing of their home, which they yearn for. They sing of their cage, which imprisons them." She put her hand over her heart and looked at me for a moment. "I understand their yearnings. I feel them here."

Yum—Breakfast in the Harem

This is definitely the easiest part of the day. There's very little preparation involved. The girls drink strong tea when they arise, and they feast on feta cheese, jams, olives, honey, and rich clotted cream. These creams and cheeses are expensive. They're hand-delivered to the royal palace by special merchants.

Technically, the servants are not supposed to eat these delicacies, but we do. There's a ridiculous amount of food served here and an abundance left over. Hegai turns his head the other way as long as we eat after the girls have had their fill.

Meals are carried from the royal kitchen to the harem by a parade of eunuchs. It's quite a sight to behold. They gracefully hoist great brass platters above their heads and walk single file into the room. The platters are placed in the center of the room on low tables covered with velvet cloth.

Today I set out the embroidered silk napkins. They're wrapped in rings made of mother-of-pearl and diamonds. I felt a little weak in the knees as I set the table. I think my jaw must have dropped, because Sohelia gave me a jab in the ribs!

Once the platters are in place, the girls help themselves to lunch or dinner, whichever the case may be. There's usually pastry filled with meat, cheese, or spinach; rice seasoned with fragrant saffron; and eggplant cooked in olive oil. There's salad made with cucumbers and broad beans, melons that burst with juice, and pomegranates sliced open to reveal their sweet, red flesh.

I'm hungry just writing about it! Pickled grapes are set out, as well as mulberries, plums, dates, figs, apples, oranges, apricots, pistachios, olives, and cheeses. I have to catch my breath; I can't possibly name all the food.

All of the girls have very healthy appetites! Esther, I noticed, is always discreet. She eats in a normal, healthy way. She doesn't deny herself, but she doesn't stuff herself either. This isn't a common characteristic among the rest of the girls. Sohelia is proud of Esther. "She's a good girl, that one," she says. "See the others? If their bellies get any rounder, we'll have to roll them into the baths."

I have to admit, it's hard to not overeat in the harem. There's always food around, especially sweets. All the girls love *gaz*, and it's served every evening. It's made from the juice of the tamarisk tree and mixed with pistachios. Then there's fig paste, almond pastries, pomegranate jellies, little cakes, and fruits cooked in syrups until they are thick and sweet.

The food is eaten with the fingers, as is the custom. "Taste is first experienced through the fingertips," my grandmother told me when I was a little girl. Didn't everyone learn this? I was surprised at the number of girls in the harem who have very bad table etiquette.

Three fingertips of the right hand are used to pick up the food. The left hand never handles food but is used instead for unclean tasks. Esther's hand glides in such a way that I'm reminded of a dance. Sohelia watched, satisfied. It's as though Esther was born to be a queen.

When the meal was over, I carried in a silver pitcher and basin. I poured the cool water over

Esther's fingers as she washed. Little towels embroidered with gold and silver were used to dry her hands.

The Bathhouse Stinks . . .

Yet we had to spend the entirety of today there.

Yes, the bathhouse! I had a sinking feeling in the pit of my stomach as I walked through the corridor and down several rows of narrow stone steps. I told myself that it was silly to be so uptight about a ghost tale. It didn't work. The feeling of foreboding clung to me.

The bathhouse is below ground because the water is stored in enormous cisterns. It's kept warm by the burning of weeds, thorn bushes, dried manure, straw, and even animal bones and carcasses.

A huge pool of water is in the center of this enormous cavern. I stopped for a moment and stared at it. Was this where the eunuch found the beautiful girl? I shivered and turned away. Smaller baths were against the walls. Water fell into each one from a pipe in the stone wall above it.

We stepped into our clogs right away. I'm so grateful for these tall wooden shoes worn only in the bathhouse. Otherwise, our feet would be on the slimy marble floor, which while beautiful, is so slippery when wet—and it's always wet. The wooden platforms of the shoes don't slip easily. Also, the water in the pools isn't changed very often. It's not uncommon to see unidentifiable objects floating in the stagnant water beside the pools. The height of the shoes keeps our feet above the water. I, for one, don't want to step in it.

I admired Esther's shoes as she slipped her small feet into them. Hegai recently gave Esther a beautiful pair. They're studded with mother-of-pearl and sapphires. She walks in them as elegantly as if she were gliding on a cloud. Oh, to be that graceful!

My clogs are plain, as are most of the servants'. I have worn bath shoes all of my life, but I wasn't born with grace. I'm clumsy and, much to my embarrassment, I sometimes stumble.

I learned a painful lesson today. It's no easy

task to bathe a girl in the harem. They're scrubbed for hours with shredded wheat biscuits. This process removes the dead, dry cells and brings the blood to the surface of the skin. At least that's what Sohelia said. Between you and me, my little diary, it looks rather like torture.

Next, olive oil, cloves, and ginger are gently rubbed over the girls' bodies. Esther endured each phase of the bath with a smile and a gentle squeeze of my hand. My admiration for her grows with each passing day.

Sohelia led Esther and me to the perfume pit in the corner of the bathhouse. A hole had been dug and filled with the smoking embers of frankincense, myrrh, and sandalwood. Esther crouched over the pit, and I arranged her robes around her to form a tent. The heat from the embers opened her pores and allowed the perfume to seep into her skin and hair. Through the process her entire body was perfumed and purified. Although I don't believe it, Persians believe this ritual wards off evil spirits.

When Esther had been thoroughly scrubbed,

perfumed, and purified, Sohelia made a paste of crushed almonds and sweet-scented jasmine. She picked up the mixture with her fingers and rubbed it over Esther's face. "This is to whiten the skin," she explained. "A white face is a sign of beauty and purity."

I brought Esther a warmed robe and wrapped her in it. Sohelia poured essence over her hair. She twisted Esther's hair up on top of her head and covered it with an embroidered cloth. Finally, perfumed water was sprinkled over her hands and face.

At last it was time for lunch! The girls ate and then collapsed on divans covered with the softest coverlets imaginable. They slept for hours, and this gave me a chance to rest as well. I had no idea that so much effort was made to look beautiful.

I'm So Tired of the Gossip and Yet...

This morning I noticed several of the girls talking excitedly among themselves. They're always whispering in little groups, and I usually don't pay any attention to them.

Today, though, I heard Esther's name mentioned. I tried to get close enough to hear them.

"Did you see him?" Leyla said. "He's always there. He walks back and forth near the courtyard every day."

"He's looking for Esther," said Zeynah. She reached for a tortoiseshell comb and ran it through her long, red locks. "His name is Mordecai. He's a Jew. What would a Jew want with a Persian girl?"

"Jews and Persians marry all the time," said Leyla. "But I heard something interesting the other day. One of the girls told me Shaashgaz overheard a conversation between two maids. He heard that Mordecai is Esther's cousin! That would make her a Jew as well."

I knew it. The other night, in the hall, there had been someone there! It was obviously Shaashgaz, a eunuch in the harem. Had he followed me? If Leyla and Zeynah had heard the rumor, who else had?

I watched the girls stare at one another, then

burst out in giggles. "That's ridiculous!" Zeynah told Leyla. "What would a Jewish girl be doing here now? It can't be true. Mordecai is probably just in love!"

"Yes," agreed Leyla. "Doesn't he know he'll never get past Sumbul?" They laughed some more, and I moved away.

The girls are right about Sumbul. He's the guard of the harem, and he always stands just outside the entrance. He's quite glorious to look at, actually. He wears a gold silk tunic that falls to his feet and is tied with a bright red sash. His outer robe is black with red trim, and he wears the customary head wrap. It's off-white with stripes of green and red. A silken plume from a black heron is tucked into a fold of his turban.

He looks very stern, but the axe he carries is even more disturbing. Mordecai has no chance of getting word to Esther through him.

Later

I found Esther peering through the latticework. "Susiana," she whispered when she saw me.

"Can I trouble you to do me a great favor?"

"Of course," I replied. "I'm at your service. What can I do for you?"

Esther looked uncomfortable. "Susiana, in addition to being my maid, I feel that you're also my friend." She hesitated. "We have a special kinship. Do you understand what I mean?"

I looked into Esther's eyes. I knew she was taking a big chance. She obviously knew I was a Jew; I didn't try to hide it. Jews in the palace are allowed to observe the Sabbath each week. She was telling me, without actually telling me, that she was a Jew. I didn't dare question her openly, though. "Yes, Esther," I replied slowly. "I do understand."

She sighed deeply and smiled. I could tell she was relieved. She took my hand. "I need to get a message to someone who is very worried about me. He paces back and forth each day just outside the courtyard. He's a special friend. "

I nodded. "Yes, I've heard about him. Would you like me to get a message to him, Esther?"

"Oh, yes, Susiana," she said excitedly.

"Could you?" She pressed a yellow handkerchief into my hand. "If you could find a way to get this to him, he'll know that I'm well."

The handkerchief was folded into a tiny square, and I quickly tucked it deep into the pocket of my robe. I'd heard about these handkerchiefs not long after I entered the harem. Since the women can't communicate directly with the outside world, they sometimes arrange for their handkerchiefs to be smuggled out. Sometimes they're given as gifts, wrapped around pieces of fruit or bundles of nuts.

The color of the handkerchief is usually a message from the gift giver. Each color has a different meaning. A red handkerchief indicates that the girl is hopelessly in love. Orange sends a message of heartache. Pink means there's a love bond. Purple indicates that the girl suffers from love. Blue means the giver hopes to be united with the person soon. If a black handkerchief is given, the girl is very lonely.

If Esther wants to give a yellow handkerchief to Mordecai, then the color yellow must be a symbol of well-being. How would I get it to him? I could never deliver anything to an officer at the king's gate without attracting attention to myself.

I must remember Father's words and let them come to me. "If you are chosen, you are equipped to do the job."

Yes, I will have the message delivered somehow. With God's help I will find a way. I must.

I've Met the Bundle Women

It's been one week since I last wrote. I'm happy to report that the answer to my dilemma has been delivered to me! In the strangest fashion, mind you. This morning Sohelia announced that we would receive visitors into the harem. This is practically unheard of!

"It's not that unusual Susiana," she told me. "We sometimes allow the merchants to bring their wares into the harem. We're in need of materials, and we won't be making a trip to the market for several weeks."

Sumbul allowed the merchants to enter. There were three women, and I knew immediately by their dress that they were Jewish. Sohelia saw me take inventory of them. "Yes, they're Jews," she said to me. "They're the only merchants admitted into the harem. They have excellent goods, they're honest, and they have fair prices."

One of the bundle women, as we call them, unloaded her goods in front of Esther and Sohelia. Layers of silk, satin, and velvet fabric were spread out on the divans. Esther ran her hand over the smooth fabrics

Lace, ribbons, and handkerchiefs were spread upon another divan. As Sohelia picked up a piece of silk and examined the fabric, the merchant slid her hand beneath the pile and pulled out a handkerchief. It was pale white. She brought it to me and pressed it into my hand. "I believe your Esther would enjoy this one," she said with a slight smile. The woman was unusual. She was very kind, but there was something in her eyes I couldn't quite read.

I moved away and opened up my hand. I turned over the handkerchief and noticed very small writing in the corner. It was in Hebrew. It read, *"Yesh hoda-ot bishvili,"* which means "Are there any messages for me?" I was so surprised that I nearly dropped the handkerchief. Mordecai had obviously had contact with the merchant before she entered the palace. She must've agreed to deliver a message from Esther to him.

I stuffed it into my pocket and pulled out the yellow one from Esther. Thankfully, no one noticed; there was far too much activity. Fabrics and other goods were passed from one set of hands to the next. Sohelia was discussing prices with the merchant, the girls were chattering excitedly, and the eunuchs were examining the wares.

I reached for a small pastry from a silver tray and placed it upon the yellow handkerchief Esther had given to me. Then I offered it to the same merchant. "If you would be so kind as to enjoy a sweet while you're here," I said.

The woman deftly popped the little pastry into her mouth and slid the handkerchief into her robe. She also reached into my pocket. Before I knew it, she had retrieved the white handkerchief as well. There! The deed was done! At least I hoped it was.

We Prepare for the Sabbath

I left the harem yesterday just before sundown, because the Sabbath begins at sundown on Friday and continues through sundown on Saturday. How glad I am that the Jews who work in the palace are always given the Sabbath, which is a day of rest, off work. We're not allowed to do any work. Preparing food, washing or mending of clothes—all of it has to be done prior to the Sabbath.

I always spend the day with Mother and Father, and I'm happy to be with them. Yesterday, though, I had Esther on my mind.

I could see the anguish in her eyes again. It's

like this every time I leave on the Sabbath. I hugged her and told her I'd be back in the evening. "Will you be all right?" I asked her. We've become quite close, and we talk much more freely now. I felt terrible leaving her.

She nodded, but I could see that she was miserable. "I feel like a traitor, she said softly. "Susiana, I don't have to pretend with you anymore. Since I've come, I haven't been able to properly observe the Sabbath. I say my prayers in private, but I live in fear that I'll be found out." It was the first time she had spoken openly about being a Jew.

"It won't always be this way," I whispered. "You don't have any choice. You're doing what you have to do, and God knows this."

Esther smiled. "I'm very grateful that I have someone like you in my life right now. It makes me feel much better. Thank you."

It's Been Six Months of Treatments
It won't be long now before the girls are presented to the king. What will happen? Who will

be chosen? If it's possible, Esther grows lovelier and lovelier each month.

Most of our time has been spent in the bathhouse to purify bodies and spirits.

Now we are told the last months will be
devoted to cosmetics of various sorts. This
morning, a great deal of time was spent applying
henna. It's an important Persian custom.

Sohelia taught me how to prepare it last
night. She took the dried leaves of the henna
plant and ground them into a very fine powder.
Then she sieved the powder through a muslin
cloth and mixed it with coffee to make a fine
paste. We set it aside overnight, and this morning I stirred it up. A few drops of eucalyptus oil
were added to increase its redness. Finally, the
henna was applied to Esther's hair to give it a
rich, red sheen. Sohelia also painted her nails,
hands, and feet.

The kings and noblemen in the Persian
Empire almost always use henna to redden their
hair and their beards.

I've even learned that butter has more than

one use! It makes a very good hairdressing. The soft fat is massaged into the hair to give it a lovely sheen. Sohelia has also taught me how to lengthen Esther's eyebrows with India ink, paint her eyelids, and powder her face and neck.

I retired to my bedchamber earlier than usual this evening. I have to get some rest. Sohelia told me that tomorrow we'll take the girls to the Grand Bazaar in the heart of Susa. Out! Can you believe it? Except for the time I've spent in the gardens and courtyards, I haven't been out of the palace since I moved into the harem. I can hardly wait.

We're Going to the Exotic Grand Bazaar

We awakened at sunrise to prepare for our adventure. I've never heard such a buzz of excitement in the harem, and why shouldn't there be? These girls hadn't left the palace either since they arrived nearly a year ago.

Esther has asked me to stay close to her today. She said, "I enjoy your company. I don't trust the other girls."

I helped her dress in a simple pink robe. It was lined in white satin and trimmed in velvet and tassels. While it was very pretty, it was simple by harem standards.

The girls always dress the most beautifully when they're within the confines of the harem. They don't want to attract too much attention when they're out. Persian men are very jealous of their women. The girls are considered prizes, and the men don't want anyone else to see their beautiful prizes.

I find this custom interesting, because my family isn't this way. Jewish women are never hidden. The men are so proud of their wives or daughters that they want other people to see them. It makes them proud when others know they have beautiful wives or sisters or daughters.

Esther's face and neck were covered with a scarf, and great care was taken to cover her nose. Only women of ill repute allow their noses to show, Sohelia told me. The only parts of Esther's body that were visible were her beautiful eyes and her graceful hands. I thought about how strange this must be for her. But now we are off . . .

Later

We left through the carriage gate—a long procession of carriages. I was fortunate to be with Esther. Since she held a high rank in the harem, we rode in the front. All of the carriages had drawn curtains so the women would not be seen. I admit that I did try to peek out, but Sohelia rebuked me so sharply that I didn't try again.

The eunuchs rode on horseback and led the parade. I could see their elegant silhouettes on both sides of the procession.

I knew we were heading due west on the Royal Road. All the royal officials travel on this road because it's so safe. Soldiers are stationed in watchtowers over the entirety of it. We hadn't been traveling very long when we reached the center of Susa, where the bazaar is located. I have been here many times with Mother and Father, and it's always been one of my favorite trips.

Esther reached into her velvet bag and took out a small hand mirror. She made sure her veil was adjusted properly, and then she checked mine! Sometimes I wonder who takes care of whom! I've noticed that she's very maternal and protective of those she cares for. It doesn't seem to matter to her in the least that I'm her maid. In her eyes, everyone is the same, and she treats them accordingly.

We wove our way through the streets, moving closer to the bazaar. Its enormous domes and cupolas can be seen from any vantage point in the city and even far beyond.

Finally, we left the safety of the carriages, surrounded by the watchful eyes of our ever-present eunuchs. I can't imagine what a picture we made—dozens of girls all dressed in identical pink robes. I forgot to mention that the girls are required to dress exactly alike when they go out. This way, none of them stand out and attract too much attention.

When we entered, I heard Esther catch her breath. It was impossible to not be in awe. At the top of the dome was an opening, which allowed the sun to seep in and spread its rays. They bounced from skylight to skylight and through the jeweled glass. The entire bazaar was bathed in a flickering glow of amber, crimson, and orange. We continuously moved through shadows, into the light and back again.

As the girls walked through the merchant stalls, everyone turned to stare. Esther immediately held up her fan to shield her veiled face. All the girls did. I don't think they realized that even their fans drew attention; they are so exquisite. Some are made of ostrich feathers and some of peacock feathers. Some are inlaid with emeralds, diamonds, and rubies. The handles are usually tortoiseshell or mother-of-pearl.

The smells of the bazaar are overpowering. They mingle together in the nostrils, not always happily. There's the sawdust that covers everything like a thin veil and the dung from the horses, mules, donkeys, and camels. There are the musky perfumes and the sweet spices, the days-old sweat and the dirty straw. There are flowers and sugarcoated candies, frosted pastries, and Arabian coffee. There's new leather, as well as the tobacco smoke that curls around long, wooden pipes. It's pleasant and repulsive all at once.

Anyone who has ever been to the bazaar will never forget this experience. I haven't been for several years, yet it's a familiar smell I never forget.

Esther, Sohelia, and I held hands and moved together, afraid to lose one another in the crowd. We paused to admire the perfumers' bottles lined up in rows. Some of the slender containers that the women call alabastrons were filled with nard and frankincense. They'd been carried on the trade caravans from India and Arabia, and they were very expensive. Others contained less expensive cinnamon oil or rose water.

Esther was happier than I'd ever seen her. Her eyes danced, and I could see a faint outline of a smile beneath her veil. She squeezed my hand and put her head close to mine. "It's been such a long time, Susi," she told me. "I've missed my freedom dearly. This is the most wonderful day."

We touched the textiles and watched the weavers pass the shuttles of their looms side to side and over and under. Everything begged to be caressed, tasted, smelled, or heard. We watched the tanner beat his hides and the artisan weave her baskets. We paused by the orchestra and watched the musicians play the harp, the flute, the dulcimer, and the lute.

We passed a flower stall, and Esther stopped to admire the flowers. Susa is famous for its lilies, which grow wild on the banks of the Choaspes River. Esther reached for two tall stalks topped with snow-white lilies and handed the woman a silver coin from her purse. She gave one to me and one to Sohelia.

I carried the flower with me all day and hoped I could get it in water before it wilted.

Even so, I would dry it and tuck it in my diary when I got back to the palace. I would keep it forever as a gift from my friend Esther and a reminder of our special day together.

The eunuchs informed us that it was time to leave. We slipped back into our carriages and bounced gently down the road, lost in our thoughts. Sohelia sat between Esther and me, and she touched both of our hands and pointed toward the curtain. We could see the silhouette of the sun as it sank slightly into the horizon. The moon hovered close.

"When I was a little girl," Sohelia said, "my mother used to sing an old Persian song to me. Her voice was lovely. She would take me outside on a night just like this, and she would point to the sky. Then she would sing, 'Last night I dreamt that the sun and moon kissed each other.'"

We watched until the sun faded away. Then the moon rose full and bright and guided us back to our palace.

It's My Birthday!

I awoke today to a gentle nudge. Esther sat on my bed with a huge smile on her face. "Wake up! It's a special day for you, Susiana!"

I sat up quickly and rubbed my eyes. A special day? Oh yes! It was my thirteenth birthday. How did Esther know? I didn't remember telling anyone.

"Dress quickly," she said. "There are many special surprises for you!"

I sat on my bed for a few minutes after she left. I knew I'd be able to see Mother and Father today, and I was sure I'd see Roxana. She never forgot my birthday. I felt happy. Birthdays always make me happy. Everyone looks at you like you are special, and they do special things for you. Last year Mother and Father took me to the river and we had a picnic on the grassy bank. I loved that.

I dressed and walked to the inner courtyard. I passed Hegai, and much to my surprise, he smiled at me. This really was a special day. I'd never seen Hegai smile before. Esther and Sohelia and some of the other maids were seated together on the divans. When they saw me, they jumped up. "Come here! Sit near us," Sohelia said. "You can't be alone today."

Persians believe that evil spirits lurk near a person on her birthday. To get rid of the evil spirits, they surround the person all day and try to bring her as much joy and laughter as they can. They believe this will chase the evil spirits away.

Of course, I don't believe in this, but Father taught me to respect their ways and try to understand their customs. After all, he said, most of them try hard to respect our ways. I didn't want to insult Sohelia. Besides, it was nice that everyone paid so much attention to me!

Sohelia knew I'd be gone all day, so she brought me a tray of sweets. It was early in the morning, but since it was my birthday, I ate them for breakfast. Of course, they were all my favorite things. How did she know? Esther watched me with great pleasure, but she was impatient and excited.

"Have you finished now?" she asked. I nodded. I was just a little sick. "I have a small gift for you on your special day, Susiana," she said. She pulled out a white handkerchief with scalloped edges. On one end, the name Hadassah was embroidered in yellow.

Esther had a tear in her eye. "My mother and father died when I was a little girl," she whispered. "As I believe you already know, I was raised by my cousin. He was very good to me, and he loved me very much. He gave me this handkerchief when I turned thirteen."

She held it out to me. "God has given me a new name now, and he has called me to serve him in a different way. I want you to have this on your thirteenth birthday so you will remember me always." Esther hugged me, and I hugged her back. I put the handkerchief in my pocket. "Go now to your mother and father. Have a wonderful day!"

As I had hoped, Roxana was waiting for me when I left the harem. "Happy birthday!" she squealed and hugged me. "Come on, we have to go to the garden. There's a surprise!"

Mother and Father clapped when they saw me. They were standing beside my birthday chair. This little chair has been in our family for as long as I can remember. When a child has a birthday in our family or in another Jewish family, a chair is always decorated with fresh flowers and greenery. I'm not a child anymore, but I'm not ready to give up this tradition. I sat in the chair, and Mother and Father lifted it thirteen times to celebrate each year of my life. Then they lifted it once more for good luck.

I noticed they were panting this time when they were finished. "Susi," Mother laughed, "this may be the last year we can lift you on the chair. You're far too big!"

Father had picked oranges and walnuts, my favorites, and Mother had prepared some special dishes in honor of my birthday. Roxana had made me a birthday crown of grapevine intertwined with flowers. We talked and told stories of my childhood and laughed. That night I slept in the apartment with Mother and Father, and I felt like that little girl again. I loved it. It was the most wonderful day.

Why the Eavesdropping?

Hegai told Sohelia that the time had come to order new clothes for Esther. The other girls will have clothes made up too, but everyone knows that Hegai has a special fondness for Esther.

I heard the girls talking again and made a point of listening. Actually, I hid behind a large pillar and eavesdropped.

"I can't stand her!" said Moj. "She thinks she's so perfect. She doesn't even talk to the rest of us."

Moj lounged by the pool, sipping a cup of sugared water. A mint leaf floated at the top.

"What about the way Hegai treats her?" added Leyla. "It's so unfair. He gives her everything. Special food! Now I hear she'll have special clothes. I think he actually wants her to become queen."

Moj laughed. "She'll never be queen. She's not like us. There's something very odd about her."

"Well, Moj," said Zeynah, "you could always trip her. You have a habit of tripping girls. Or she could have an accident in the bath-house and end up dead like that other one. What was her name?"

The girls laughed wickedly now. "That was just a ghost story, Zeynah," said Moj, mocking a shocked looked. "Or was it?"

They laughed some more; I felt uneasy. I had to keep a close eye on Esther, and I had to be careful not to be followed anymore. Who knew what Shaashgaz had heard?

The Dressmaker Has Arrived

It looks like she'll stay for a while too. She'll take all of the girls' measurements, and that won't be a short or easy task. They were already measured once and fitted for a wardrobe when they arrived. Unfortunately, most of the girls haven't retained their shapes. It's just as Sohelia predicted. They ate too many sweets, and now they can't fit into their clothes.

Sohelia offered a word of wisdom to the harem today. "While it's better to be a bit plump than too skinny," she announced, "no man, especially a king, wants a fat queen."

The girls acted a little insulted when she said this. They're being put on strict diets, but they're running out of time. Besides, it's rumored that they hide food and eat it in the middle of the night. In that case, no one can help them.

More Surprises Abound

The hustle and bustle in the harem has increased considerably. Earlier today the Jewish merchants were welcomed into the secret chambers once again. The same bundle woman who delivered Esther's yellow handkerchief to Mordecai delivered luxurious fabrics. "Come," she said to Esther. "Tell me what you like."

While Esther pored over the cloths, she asked her casually, "Still well?" Esther smiled and nodded. Another message delivered. Hegai and Sohelia also looked at the fabrics. In the end, they chose bolts of red satin, gold velvet, crimson and white silk, and so many others that I can't remember. I don't know how Esther will wear all these garments at once to impress the king, but maybe they know something I don't. I'll wait and see.

We're Going to See the Puppeteers

The idea came from all the tension in the harem that grows thicker as the day to visit the king draws near. The girls are moody, solemn, and argumentative. I thank God every day that I attend Esther and not one of the others. I don't know what I'd do if that were the case.

I have developed the peculiar habit of moving about like a spy. I hide behind a pillar and peek out to make sure the coast is clear. Then I move stealthily across the room and am prepared to duck and take cover in an instant. It's not uncommon these days to see mirrors flying across the room and personal belongings adrift in the pool.

Hegai sends any hot-tempered girls to the

outer courtyard to cool down. In the meantime, he's finally come to the conclusion that the atmosphere must be lightened. He's decided to have a troupe of professional shadow puppeteers come and put on a show.

A large piece of transparent muslin cloth was hung from a silver bar and illuminated by candles. A painting of a wedding banquet was hung upon the cloth. Then the center was cut out to accommodate the shadow puppets. A long piece of velvet covered the table and hid the bodies of the mysterious puppeteers.

It was a silly show, but entertaining. It was especially funny when a gazelle ran under the table and pulled the velvet cloth with him as he ran away. The whole show lasted more than an hour, and in the end we all laughed and laughed. It was a good break, and everyone felt better for it.

The New Clothes Are Being Fitted

Sohelia decided it was in Esther's best interest

not to let the other girls see her gowns and dress-es. Actually, it was in our best interests as well. We were all tired of listening to the girls bicker. When the dressmaker came, she took Esther into a private chamber and had her try on everything to make sure it fit perfectly. All is well, I sup-pose, because she left and Esther emerged with a half smile on her face.

I sat beside her next to the golden cage of nightingales. These birds seemed to comfort her so, and now I find that they are strangely com-forting to me as well. "Well," I asked, "how were they? Beautiful?"

When Esther looked at me, she seemed to stare right through me. "Oh yes," she mur-mured. "They're extraordinary. Exquisite. Without a doubt the most beautiful fabric that has ever touched my skin."

Esther seemed strangely distant. Her fingers moved in little circles upon her lap, over and over again. It wasn't a habit I'd noticed before. Without thinking I reached out and put my hand over them. "Esther? Is something wrong?"

She stared away for several moments. "Susi," she began, "I'm not sure what it is. I feel strange. Part of me is excited, but I'm not sure why. Part of me is afraid, but I'm not sure why."

We sat quietly and watched the birds frolic. They usually hopped from one golden pedestal to another, but they were strangely still tonight. I wished I could open the cage and set them free. I'd love to watch them spread their wings and fly away.

I couldn't think of the right words to tell Esther. I spent many sleepless nights pondering. Would Esther become our next queen? If not, what would become of her? Would she stay in the harem? What would become of me? Why was I here? There are certainly maids much more qualified than me. Was it all part of God's plan?

The questions never stopped in my mind. I can't imagine the questions Esther must have. She was a simple Jewish girl who somehow ended up in a palace. Was it possible she was being groomed to become the next queen of the

Persian Empire? It was really quite unbelievable.

"Esther, I believe there are things going on
that we have no control over. It's as if someone
is guiding our paths." Of course, I was referring
to God, but I had to be careful about what I said.
I never knew if someone was hiding behind the
folds of a drapery, listening.

"I can't really explain it," I told her. "I just
know that it's coincidental that we are both—"

"Shhh," she whispered and put a hand gently over my mouth. She put her arm around me
and pulled me close. "We just have to believe,
Susiana. We just have to believe. We will have
our answers soon enough."

I've Been Shaken Today

I awoke with a start this morning to find someone standing beside my bed. I nearly jumped out
of my skin, but the figure seemed familiar to me
even in my sleepy state. My eyes began to
adjust, and I realized it was Sohelia.

"I'm sorry, Susi," she apologized, "but I have just been informed that the girls will be presented to His Royal Highness King Xerxes today."

I nearly fell out of bed trying to untangle myself from my coverlets. "What? When? I mean, all of them? How? Why today?" I felt panic begin to rise up in my throat.

"Calm down," Sohelia said. Then I noticed that she was wringing her hands.

I sat back down on my bed and just stared at her. "Sohelia?" She just looked at me. "Are you nervous?" I had never seen her nervous before. She was always the picture of calm.

She realized she'd let her guard down, and she immediately became more businesslike. I think she was embarrassed. "Of course not, Susiana. Why would I be nervous? I'm not going before the king."

I smiled. I liked her this way. It showed me that she cared for Esther—apparently a great deal. "Oh," I said. "You wouldn't be nervous for Esther by any chance, would you?"

Sohelia just shook her head in exasperation. "Come when you're ready. We have a great deal to do. We must pick out her outfit and her jewels, her hair must be readied, her cosmetics must be applied. Oh dear." Then she fluttered out of the room.

Now I have to get dressed. I wish Roxana were here to help me with my hair today. I'm in no mood to mess with it.

I'm Beside Myself

Esther left this evening to visit King Xerxes. She went on Hegai's arm. I hardly know what to say or do; I'm so nervous. In recent months I have developed the terrible habit of biting my nails. It's completely unacceptable, Sohelia tells me, and I know it. Although she's really one to talk! Sohelia has paced the halls since Esther left, and she even mumbles to herself! Anyway, it's true that my fingernails have been chewed to the quick, and they look positively awful. I try to hide them as much as possible, but it's a challenging task when I use them as much as I do. It's a habit I must break.

Esther looked beautiful when she left. I felt so proud of her. Her black hair gleamed with the emeralds Sohelia had carefully woven into her long braid. Her skin shone; her eyes were wide and bright.

She wore a green silk caftan. A matching waistcoat was fitted snugly to her body, and it was decorated with green and gold fringe. Her loose robe was embroidered with gold. Her ears were hung with diamonds larger than walnuts! Rows of smaller but equally translucent diamonds adorned her head scarf.

Hegai had chosen everything, and he'd done a magnificent job.

I truly believe that Esther could have worn a rag and it wouldn't have made a difference. The jewels and clothing certainly added to her beauty, but they didn't make her beautiful. I was reminded of what Esther told me about the colorful plumage of the parrots and the macaws. Anyone can wear beautiful clothes, but what's within the person? It was that beauty that shone from her eyes, and it was that beauty that the other girls knew they couldn't compete against.

Some of them, such as Moj, Leyla, and Zeynah, have already visited the king. They'll probably remain in the harem, but their chances to succeed Queen Vashti to the throne are slim. It's what I hear again and again. Every day the girls go with expectation, and every day they return, their hopes dashed.

It's late in the night now, and still Esther hasn't returned. I don't believe she will until the morning. I'll lie on this divan near her nightingales and wait for her. I'm surprised that Sohelia hasn't scolded me and told me to sleep in my own bed. I think she feels sorry for me.

The winter rains have arrived with a surprising ferocity. As I write, they pound their wet fists against the windows. The brick walls of the castle harbor little warmth, and I can feel the damp air settle into my bones.

I've pulled the silky coverlets around me snugly and made a nice little cocoon for myself.

The harem is strangely quiet. Even the nightingales sing their soulful songs more softly this evening. Nearly everyone is asleep in their beds. The fountains trickle peacefully; the candles flicker and create their own shadow puppets on the wall. I see a silver streak of lightening, then another. I'll close my eyes. It's an odd, lonely night.

Excited Voices

I awoke just after sunrise to the low murmur of voices, wondering why everyone was awake so early. Something was happening again. I could feel it in the air. Then I walked into the hall and saw Sohelia already walking toward my bedchamber.

She took my hands in her own. "Susiana, I have news for you," she said. "Wondrous news."

I knew then. "Esther!" I exclaimed. "It's about Esther, right?"

Sohelia nodded her head very quickly.

"Xerxes has chosen her?"

Sohelia only beamed and nodded again. It was as if she couldn't speak. Her full mouth was drawn into a tight line, and I realized the ever-strong, stoic Sohelia was trying not to cry!

"You mean she's queen?" I knew it and yet at the same time couldn't believe it. "Esther, our Esther, is the new queen?"

"Yes, yes, Susi!" Sohelia cried. "Esther is queen." Sohelia hugged me tight and smiled now. It was a deep, deep smile, and it didn't leave her face for a long time.

"The king has placed the royal crown upon her head and proclaimed her queen," Sohelia said. "In seven days there will be a huge banquet to celebrate their marriage. That is when she'll be introduced to all the nobles and officials as the new queen of Persia."

"What of the other girls, Sohelia?" I asked. "What will become of them?"

"The best ones shall remain," she told me. "They'll become Xerxes' secondary wives."

The Royal Proclamation Was Amazing

At the first light of dawn, the royal couriers were dispatched. They flew from the palace and thundered down the road to deliver the royal proclamation that Esther has been proclaimed queen. They also carried banquet invitations, which were delivered to thousands of noblemen and officials within the province.

The Persian couriers are famous for their quickness. There's a courier and horse stationed along every stop of the Royal Road, equal to the number of days the journey will take. That means if it were to take two days to get to Persipolis, a fresh courier and horse would be waiting at the end of the first day's journey. It is said that nothing can stop these couriers. Not darkness, nor heat, nor rain, nor snow.

Diary Two
The Days of Esther, Our Queen

478 B.C.

This Isn't a Dream...

And so I've decided to start a new diary for the days of Queen Esther!

Esther returned this afternoon, and she'll move into a separate apartment within the harem. At least I don't have to move again! Her return is a joyous one. She greeted Hegai warmly and then ran to hug Sohelia and me.

I'm still having trouble acknowledging all that has happened, so I stuttered and stammered upon seeing my queen. "Esther, . . . I mean Queen Esther, . . . I mean Your Royal Highness," I said, then, finally giving up, "What should I call you now?"

"Susi, you must still call me Esther," she said firmly. "Oh, and by the way, I've appointed you and Sohelia official attendants to the queen. Now we'll never be separated."

Sohelia left to make sure Esther's apartment was ready. This left Esther and me alone for a few minutes. We went outside to the courtyard and sat on a bench. There was a definite chill in the air, and I pulled my robe more snugly around me. I tried to conceal my glances at her. I wondered if she had changed.

"Esther," I said slowly. "You are our queen. You are my queen. You are queen to everyone in Persia." I didn't know if I was talking to Esther or to myself.

But Esther shook her head. "I feel as if I'm in a dream," she said in her same kind way. No, she hadn't changed. "Nothing seems real. It doesn't seem bad, but it doesn't necessarily seem good either. It just feels like all of this is happening to someone else and I'm in the audience watching it. Like in a play."

I had to ask her. There was no one around us. My words wouldn't go anywhere. "Does King Xerxes know?" I said softly.
"Are you asking me if he knows I'm a Jew?" She mouthed the word Jew.

"Yes," I replied.

She shook her head again. "Then the answer is no, Susi. He doesn't know."

"Will you be safe?" I asked. Things had

changed now. Everything seemed much more serious. The stakes were higher. She was no longer just a Jewish girl in the harem. She was the first Jewish queen of Persia, and no one in the royal court even knew.

"Esther, what if someone finds out," I pressed. "I mean, if the king finds out, won't he be angry?"

I thought about Queen Vashti. If Xerxes had banished her for her disobedience, what would he do to Esther if he believed she'd lied to him?

Esther took my hand. "We know someone who knows more than we do, Susi." She was obviously referring to God. "I am completely baffled as to why I'm here—why I was chosen. It's beyond my ability to comprehend. Please remember, though, that I wasn't the only one chosen."

"What do you mean, Esther?" I asked.

"Do you think it's coincidental that you're here with me?" she asked. I'd thought of this before, many times. "It's not a coincidence," she answered. "You're here for a reason, as am I.

We'll know more when it's the right time for us to know."

She was right. That night she hugged me before she went into her new apartment for the evening. "No worries," she said to me. "Promise me you won't worry, and I'll do the same for you."

"I promise you that I'll try," I offered. It was the best I could do.

Esther's Banquet Began Today

According to established tradition, most royal banquets continue for at least two weeks, so we may be celebrating for a while. The celebration began in the palace, but now it's to be carried out throughout the entire Persian Empire. There's great merriment in every town and in every province, especially in Susa.

Thousands of people have gathered in the streets. We can hear their voices from within the palace walls, which is remarkable. "Long live the queen! Long live the queen!" they shout.

Sohelia and I left the harem and were peeking through doorways and around columns, trying to catch a glimpse of King Xerxes and Esther. I saw Roxana in the corridor, and she joined us.

There's a wide, inky moat that snakes around the high, red walls of the palace. The guests must walk over a bridge and climb the double staircase that converges at the top of the limestone terrace. The steps are very shallow and wide so that horses can easily climb them. King Xerxes and Esther greeted the noblemen and dignitaries at the top of these steps. The guests continued on to the banquet after passing through the Gate of Xerxes. Two enormous and fearsome stone bulls guard the gate.

"Look Roxana, isn't he magnificent?" I said.

I was referring to King Xerxes. His long beard was tightly curled and henna red. His scarlet robes were edged with sable, and a solid-gold, fluted crown sat neatly upon his head. A diamond-encrusted dagger hung from his waist.

In his right hand he carried his royal scepter. It was gold and had a jeweled knob. In his left hand was a lotus blossom with two buds.

"Yes," she agreed, "but look at Esther, Susi. She's magnificent. This is all like a story."

Esther did look magnificent. She wore a purple velvet dress embroidered in gold. Her crown was a simple purple ribbon with streaks of white, and she wore it around her forehead.

"You may never see Esther with the king like this again," Sohelia told us. "They aren't usually seen together officially. She's by his side now simply because it's her banquet. The guests would be disappointed today if she wasn't highly visible."

We lingered for a moment while the guests slipped out of their carriages. Some of the men wore sapphire blue robes and gold tunics. They all bore gifts. No one would dare attend a palace banquet without presenting a gift to the king.

It's well-known that Xerxes prefers gifts of gold and silver. His treasury is rumored to hold valuables piled to the ceiling. Of course, it's heavily guarded. It's also known that Xerxes gives as many gifts as he receives. His generosity with his subjects, Sohelia told me, often ensures their loyalty.

"Come," she said now. "There's work to be done."

I glanced over my shoulder as I walked. I couldn't help it. I was entranced by the splendor.

One Week Later~
Esther's Banquet Continues

The celebrations continue! Mother told me that by the end of the two weeks, fourteen thousand animals will have been slaughtered to feed the guests. Fourteen thousand! That's a lot of meat.

"What kind of animals?" I asked her warily.

"Oh, the usual," she replied. "Camels, horses, oxen, donkeys, deer, ostriches, geese."

A portion is served to all the guests. Whatever is left on their plates is carried home with them. The rest of the meat and food is served in the courtyard to the servants, including the bodyguard and the palace soldiers.

The courtyards are always beautiful, but during celebrations like these they're more than beautiful. During the day sunlight streams through glass balls filled with colored water. Rose petals float in the fountains, and canaries sing from golden cages. At night torches are lit in every corner, and musicians fill the evening air with the hypnotic notes of the flute, dulcimer, lute, and harp.

Inside the palace and throughout the province, there's a different form of entertainment every night. There are jugglers, acrobats, dancers, and even wrestlers.

Huge damask and velvet hangings of white, green, and blue hang from the seventy-foot columns in the banquet hall. The couches are upholstered with gold and silver cloth that begs the guests to recline with a gold goblet of wine. The floors are made of multicolored marble.

Wine flows freely at all palace banquets. The nobles drink a common wine, but the king drinks only wine made from the choice grapes of Chalybon. They grow on the sunny slopes above Damascus. He likes it so well that his royal chamberlain has put him to bed every evening thus far.

Banquets also serve an important military purpose by displaying the great wealth of the king. Everyone knows that if a king has great wealth, he probably has the finest army at his disposal.

Later

Well, the banquet is over, and thousands of guests have gone home. I feel rather sad about it. There was so much noise and merriment, and now it's eerily quiet by comparison. It's always disappointing after a party.

Esther is asleep in her bed. Sohelia is probably asleep too. In fact, I think most of the girls are asleep.

I believe I'd like to be asleep as well. I'm afraid this will have to be short tonight. I'm so tired I can barely hold my pen upright . . .

I'm Unsure about the Eunuch

Esther was preparing to eat her breakfast when he hurried in.

Hathach is his name and he is one of the king's eunuchs who was assigned to Esther when she became queen. He seems quite nice, but Sohelia has cautioned me to be wary of him.

"Never forget," she said sternly, "that Xerxes assigned Hathach to Esther not only to serve her but also to observe her. He'll report any disloyal behavior immediately. His first allegiance lies with the king. It's that way with all eunuchs. Remember that."

He handed Esther a note. "It was given to me by an official at the gate," he told her. "I was told it's of an urgent nature." Esther unfolded the paper. I could see alarm spread across her face as she read it.

"Thank you, Hathach," she said politely. "Please return in a few moments. I'll have something for you."

She moved with purpose to a small table.

There she opened up a drawer and took out a piece of paper. With her delicate, purposeful handwriting, she wrote at length. Sohelia looked at me with a furrowed brow then continued to watch Esther. No one said a word.

Esther folded the top third of the letter down and the bottom third up so that it overlapped. She took a small piece of rounded wax from the drawer, softened it over the yellow flame of a candle, and then sealed the letter with it. Quickly she pressed her signet ring into the wax. I marveled at it. This was the official signature of the queen.

When Hathach returned a moment later, she handed it to him. "Deliver this to the king at once. It's urgent." As he left quickly, Esther sat nervously in a chair.

Sohelia couldn't wait a moment longer. "What is it Esther?" she asked impatiently. "What's happened?"

"I'll tell you both," she said, "but you can't breathe a word of it to anyone. I was informed of a plot to kill King Xerxes."

"What?" I struggled to keep my voice low.

Sohelia looked at me crossly. "Is the source reliable?" she asked.

"Very reliable," Esther said. She looked at me for a long moment as if trying to tell me something with her eyes. What was it? She said the source was reliable, very reliable. It came to me then, and I inhaled sharply. Sohelia stared at me. The source was Mordecai. He had obviously overheard a plot to kill the king.

"Sohelia," Esther said, "what do you know of Bigthana and Teresh?"

"Oh," said Sohelia, "those two. They are two of the king's eunuchs—chamberlains they are. They're trouble, Esther. They were very loyal to Vashti, and they were upset when King Xerxes divorced her. To this day, they're very vocal about their displeasure with the king."

Esther nodded her head. "They're the ones," she said solemnly. "We can only hope that the plot has been uncovered in time. We'll have to wait and see what comes of this."

It's Late and I'm Sad

Our day plodded on slowly until finally Esther received word. The plot to kill Xerxes had been found out in time.

"The eunuchs were interviewed, and so was Mordecai," Esther told me when we were alone. "It was found to be true, of course."

"So Xerxes knows it was Mordecai who saved his life?" I asked.

"Yes, it's all recorded in the royal annals," Esther said proudly. "His name will go down in history as having saved the life of our king."

"And what about the eunuchs?" I asked her. "What will become of them?"

"Oh, that's very sad," she said softly. "They'll be hanged on the gallows at daybreak."

I sighed heavily. I know that justice has to be done, but it's still sad. The thought of anyone hanging on the gallows is unbearable. It's a particularly cruel punishment.

Why do we even call it *hanging*? The term is misleading. In actuality, a stake is set in the ground with the pointed side facing up. The victim is pushed down upon the sharp point of the stake until it plunges through his body and exits from his neck. It's horrendous.

No one deserves to die this way.

Morning

I finally found Esther in the courtyard. She was sitting on a stone bench beneath a eucalyptus tree. It's where we always go to talk, or where one of us goes when we need to think. It was cold. The leaves had turned brown months ago. They drifted on the ground in the shifting wind.

"Esther?" She was far away, lost in thought, and she didn't hear me. "Esther?" I called, a little louder this time.

She jumped. "Oh! Susi! You startled me. I was lost in a daydream." She patted the bench beside her. "Come, sit with me for a little while."

"What are you thinking about?" I asked her.

"Haman," she said.

I thought for a moment. The name sounded familiar to me. "Haman . . . Haman . . . ," I thought aloud. "I give up, Esther. Who is Haman?"

She looked at me with a darkness behind her eyes that I wasn't used to. "He was selected to be vizier to the king today. Do you know what that means?"

"I know it's an important position, a very important position, right?" I asked.

"Yes," Esther said. "He's the king's closest advisor now. His rank is higher than all of the other nobles in Persia. And he's an Agagite."

I shook my head. "An agag who?"

She picked up some leaves from beside her feet and crunched them in her hand. "An Agagite," she repeated. "They're descendants of the Amalekites, ancient enemies of the Jews. They're a bloodthirsty people. History tells us that when Moses left Egypt and camped at Rephidim, they came from the hills and attacked our people. They took our women with them or killed them along with their children."

"But that was a long time ago, Esther," I said. "What does that have to do with the Jews today and with Haman?"

"Susi, anyone with a heart bent against the Jews has a heart bent against God," Esther explained patiently. "God told King Saul to destroy the Agagites completely, and he failed to do so. They're a bad seed that hasn't been rooted out. They won't rest until every Jew is destroyed."

I felt afraid then. There was something in her words, something about her passion, that made me worried. "Esther, they can't hurt us now, can they?"

She just stared away then. "This is a time when we must trust in God. That's all I can tell you. I have an uneasy feeling inside of me, and it won't go away."

Later

Sohelia gave permission to leave the harem, so I went in search of Roxana.

I found her folding towels in the laundry. She turned when she heard footsteps.

"Susi!" she cried.

I offered her a weak smile. "Roxana, where's Damaris?" I asked.

She dropped her towel and stared at me. "Damaris?" she repeated. "There's got to be something wrong if you want to know where Damaris is."

"I have to talk to her, Roxana," I said. "If anyone knows what's going on around the palace, she does."

Luckily, Damaris wasn't that hard to find. She was on the steps headed toward the kitchen. "You want to talk to me?" she asked suspiciously. She was annoyed too.

"Damaris," Roxana said sweetly, "We were hoping you could help us. You know things that no one else knows."

Damaris smiled and stood up a little straighter. "Well, yes, I suppose that's true," she said and coughed. "Why? What's this all about?"

"I was wondering if you know anything about Haman?" I asked.

"A few things," she said evasively.

"Damaris!" I said. "This is important. What do you know?" She just looked at me; her eyes were narrowed, and her chubby arms were crossed in front of her chest.

I sighed. I had to be careful. If I wasn't nice, I wouldn't get any information out of her.

"I'm sorry," I said more softly. "It's just that I need to know. I can't explain why; you'll just have to trust me."

She stared at me with her narrow eyes, and I looked to Roxana for help. I remember thinking, *This is going to be more difficult than I thought.*

"Damaris," Roxana said. "I personally know that Susi has mentioned your name to the queen. She said you were a trusted servant and a loyal subject of His Royal Highness."

Her eyebrows shot up, and a pink blush spread across her round cheeks. "Really?" she stammered. She looked at me. "You told her that?"

"Yes, I'm sure I said something like that," I hedged.

"Well," she softened, "it's true that I'm a loyal subject."

"Very loyal," Roxana agreed. I nodded my head. "That's why you want to give us information that might help the queen."

"Well, all right," Damaris agreed, "but only if it'll help the queen. Don't let it get around that I told you."

"Never," Roxana said.

"Never," I repeated.

Damaris took a deep breath and leaned close. "I've heard, through certain channels," she whispered, "that Haman was behind that plot to kill the king."

Roxana and I looked at each other.

"There's more," she said. "Haman apparently bribed those two eunuchs. He promised them that once the king was gone, he'd promote them. They planned to slay the king in his bedchamber and poison Queen Esther."

My legs were shaky, and I sank down on the

cold stone steps. "Why?" I asked. "Why would he do such a thing?"

"He wants to be king, why else?" said Roxana.

"That's right," said Damaris. "Believe me, he's the kind that will stop at nothing to get what he wants."

Before we left, I asked Damaris to get word to me if she heard anything else. She agreed.

Maybe she isn't as bad as I've always thought.

Diary Three
Living by the King

474 B.C.

Tension Is Building in the Palace

The atmosphere feels like a pot of soup that boils at the bottom and eventually bubbles over the top. Everyone here is talking a great deal about Mordecai now.

Esther cornered Hathach the other day and asked him directly. She was gracious but intense and direct.

I heard Esther say, "I hear all manner of things in regards to the official Mordecai. Can you tell me, Hathach, what is happening?"

"It would appear," replied Hathach, "that Mordecai is the only royal official who refuses to prostrate himself before Haman. He says he won't prostrate himself before anyone except God. He finally told the other officials that he's a Jew."

Esther pondered this for a moment. "Hathach," she said slowly, "when you say 'prostrate himself,' you're not referring to merely bowing before Haman. Am I correct to assume this?"

"Yes, you are correct, Queen Esther," said

Hathach. "In fact, if it would make it clearer for you, I can tell you exactly what Mordecai said about this."

Esther was surprised. "You remember his exact words?"

"I do," Hathach said. "They made quite an impression upon me when I heard them. I was there at the time, you know."

"Well then, yes, please," said Esther.

Hathach squared his shoulders and cleared his throat and repeated Mordecai's words: "You know that if I have not adored Haman, it is not through pride or contempt or secret desire for glory. I would kiss the feet of Haman gladly for the salvation of Israel, but I fear that I will give to a man that honor which I know belongs only to my God."

I was listening while I wove pearls through Esther's braid. When Hathach finished, the room was quiet. We were lost in Mordecai's words. I knew exactly what Hathach and Esther were talking about, because I'm a Jew. Mother and Father had conversations with me about this very thing.

Jewish law doesn't forbid men or women to bow to officials. It's an act of respect used for authority figures, and it's not considered sacrilegious in any way. We practice it all the time in the palace. However, there's a huge difference between bowing and prostrating oneself.

When Hathach left, Esther turned to me. "Susi, it would appear that Haman requires his subjects to prostrate themselves in much the same way we prostrate ourselves before God. He expects them to lie down with their hands and feet stretched out and their mouths in the dust."

"I know, Esther. I understand this," I told her. "Haman must think of himself as a sort of god."

"Yes," said Esther, "and I can tell you from experience that Mordecai will never do it, especially not before Haman, whom he despises. He'll die first."

I thought about this. Mordecai showed tremendous courage and conviction to do what he did. Would I have that same courage if I were in his shoes? I'd like to think so, but would I? Perhaps I'll never know. I do know that his words have been burned into my memory. They were powerful, and I won't easily forget them.

The Month of Nisan

This is a strange month. The weather is very unpredictable. One day hot winds blow in from the east. On another day cold rains fall from the sky. On another day we could be pummeled with hailstorms. I suppose it's fitting that the strange weather outside mirrors the strange atmosphere in the palace right now.

In two weeks we will celebrate the Feast of Passover! By "we" I mean the Jews. It will be a small feast in Mother and Father's apartment. Roxana and her mother and father usually come as well. It's a time for us to remember what God has done for us.

We remember how he rescued the Jews from Egypt, and Father retells the story of the Passover. This was when the death angel crept through Egypt and killed all of the firstborn children but spared the children of the Israelites. It's a story from the pages of our history, and I've heard it every year for as long as I can remember.

We eat unleavened bread, wine, bitter herbs, and roasted lamb. I love this time. It's special to our family. It makes us feel close and very proud to be Jewish.

I only hope that when I'm there, Mother won't talk to me about marriage again. I'll be eighteen soon, and she tells me that if I'm not careful, I'll die an old, lonely maid!

I do want to marry, but right now I think it's my time to serve Esther and devote myself to her. I believe it's what God wants me to do. I still have time.

It's the Dark of Night

I awoke a bit ago to a great commotion. At first I thought I was dreaming, but I heard shouts and they persisted until I was finally awakened. The little lamp on my bedside table had burned all night. With this light I saw Sohelia run into my bedchamber.

"You must come at once, Susi," she had cried. "There's someone outside the harem—a girl, it seems. She keeps shouting your name. Sumbul is about to carry her away."

My palms were sweaty. All I could think of was Mother and Father. Were they hurt? Had someone come to deliver bad news? It was apparent that something was terribly wrong. I struggled to pull a robe over my head. I ran out my door and down the cold corridor. In my haste, I'd forgotten to slip on my shoes. Esther was coming out of her bedchamber at the same time.

"What is it? What's happened?" she asked me. "Who shouts so?" I shook my head, and we raced down the long hallway together. Many of the girls were already huddled in the hall. They whispered nervously.

As I neared the large wooden doors, the voice grew louder. It was definitely not Mother,

Sohelia, Esther, Damaris, or Roxana.

"I have to talk to her," the female shouted. "Don't you understand? This is an emergency."

Esther grabbed my hand, and she rapped loudly on the doorpost. "Sumbul, it's Esther," she said loudly. "Open the doors, please."

The doors slowly creaked open to reveal the guard. He was holding on to a large girl, who struggled wildly. I narrowed my eyes. It was hard to see in the dim light. When she stopped moving, I was able to get a clear picture of her face. I couldn't believe my eyes.

"Damaris ?" I asked.

"You know this servant, Susiana?" Esther asked me.

"Yes, I have known her for years," I said.

"Do you wish to speak with her?" Esther asked.

"Yes, of course." I practically shouted.

"I'll work something out with Sumbul," Esther told me, looking at the guard. "You'd better take her away from here right now," she said to me. "I can persuade him not to report this girl this time, but if it happens again I may be powerless to do anything for her."

I thanked Esther, kind Esther, always compassionate. I made sure to walk quickly past the guard and avoid his eyes, though I felt them boring into my back as I moved away. I was half leading, half dragging Damaris down the corridor, well out of listening range.

We turned several corners and stood close to a night lamp. It burned from a niche in the wall. I couldn't even think of what to say. *What on earth was Damaris doing here in the middle of the night?* I wondered. *And what was she shouting about?*

Damaris looked wild eyed, and her hair was disheveled. I'd never seen her like this.

"I have news to tell you," she said slowly. "Terrible news."

I felt my heart pound again. "Is it Mother and Father?" I asked her. "Is something wrong? Are they all right?" Father had not felt well for most of the year, and I was constantly worried about him.

"Oh yes, Susi," she said and touched my arm. "They're all right . . . fine for now."

"For now?" I had no patience for this. I demanded to know what she was talking about. "Spit it out," I said, grabbing her arm.

She shook her head and took a deep breath. "Susi, Haman has done a terrible thing. He was very angry with Mordecai, angrier than anyone knew. He's convinced King Xerxes to kill all the Jews in the Persian Empire."

I studied Damaris in the shadowy light. *This was ridiculous,* I thought. She had to be lying. "Why, Damaris?" I demanded. "Why would Xerxes agree to such a thing? This is crazy. No one agrees to kill an entire race of people."

Now Damaris put her hands on my shoulders and shook me. "Listen to me!" she said. "It's happened. He convinced Xerxes that the Jews are nothing but troublemakers. In the morning the royal secretaries will get out their pens and paper and write up the decree. By this afternoon the couriers will be dispatched to deliver the decree. Don't you understand? The *pur* was cast—a lot was cast. That means that on the thirteenth day of Adar, all Jews in the Persian Empire will be killed. It's a royal decree, the *pur* or lot. Nothing can stop it from taking place now."

I shook my head and ran down the corridor. "Susi!" I heard my name, but it sounded far away, like in a dream. I wanted to wake up.

Even as I record these events I wonder: How can such a terrible dream feel so real?

The Next Morning

The sky was a dark, depressing gray this morning, and the heavy clouds threatened to dump rain. The wind rattled the windows, and the cold air crept under the doors and through the cracks. I never went back to sleep after I left Damaris. I couldn't. I saw the light of Esther's lamp glowing in the corridor, but I crept past. She had waited for me, but I couldn't bear to talk to her. How would I tell her?

She would find out today, as would Mother

and Father and Roxana—if they didn't already know.

I stayed in bed until I heard footsteps and voices. I heard Sohelia first. "They say it's Mordecai. He stands just beyond the king's gate and wails bitterly. He's dressed in sackcloth, and he's covered with ashes."

I knew why Mordecai mourned, even though others in the palace didn't. How could they know our custom of tearing our clothes, dressing in sackcloth, and covering ourselves with ashes to show our distress when someone died or there was a terrible tragedy?

Of course, I couldn't bring myself to say anything just yet. It was apparent that they were about to find out anyway.

"Have clothes sent to him at once," Esther told Sohelia. "He won't be allowed to reenter the king's gate dressed in sackcloth."

A eunuch was dispatched to Mordecai with fresh clothes in his arms. A short time later, he returned with the same clothes. "He refuses the clothes," the eunuch announced. "He repeats the same words over and over again. He says, 'A people are going to be destroyed who have done no evil.'"

By now I was dressed, and I reluctantly left my bedchamber. "Please, will you find Hathach?" Esther asked Sohelia. "Ask him to go to Mordecai and find out what this means." Sohelia scurried away.

Esther was in a state unlike I had ever seen her. *"Airetai eqnov mhden hdikhkov,"* she murmured. "Susi, it's so strange. Mordecai repeats this over and over again." I watched her repeat the words under her breath. *"Airetai eqnov mhden hdikhkov.* A people are going to be destroyed who have done no evil. What does he mean by this? I can't imagine."

She paced from the window to the doors until the heavy wood swung open on its hinges and Hathach appeared. Esther waited, but Hathach didn't say anything.

"Hathach, what is it?" Esther asked him. "Please, tell me."

"It's very unsettling news, Queen Esther,"

he said and expelled a heavy sigh. "The royal couriers delivered an edict this morning. He held a piece of parchment in his hands. It would appear that King Xerxes has ordered the annihilation of every Jew in the Persian Empire—every man, every woman, every child. On the thirteenth day of the twelfth month of Adar, every Jew will be slaughtered."

Damaris had been right about all of it. I flashed back to what Esther had told me in the garden about Haman and the Agagites. Hadn't she said, "They won't rest until every Jew is destroyed?" Yes, I was sure she'd said that.

Esther just stared at Hathach. She'd believed it could happen, but now that it had, it obviously seemed unreal to her. Even Hathach was disturbed, and he wasn't even a Jew. I thought of how distraught Damaris had been last night. The destruction of thousands was ordered merely because they were Jewish?

Esther waved her hand in the air. "No! It's impossible," she told him. "You must have heard wrong."

Reluctantly, Hathach handed her the parchment, and Esther read it over. She sank into the divan nearest her. The color had drained from her face. I sat close and held her hand. "Haman?" she asked.

"Yes," Hathach said. "It would appear that Haman provided the proper support and encouragement. He also offered to pay ten thousand talents of silver to the men who carry out the business.

Esther's eyes widened. "Is that what he thinks the Jews are worth these days?" she said slowly. "Ten thousand talents of silver? The tiniest Jew alone is worth far more than that to God."

Hathach took a step toward her. "There is one more thing, I'm afraid. Mordecai has made a request." He waited until Esther looked up and fixed her attention on him.

"He has asked me to urge you to pay a visit to the king. He wants you to beg for mercy and plead with him to save the Jews."

The room grew very quiet then. Sohelia sat

with her hands in her lap. Hathach waited with his eyes averted. I looked at Esther's hand resting in my own. Her skin was cold, and I thought I felt a slight tremor. I heard the whistle of the wind as it squeezed through a crack.

"Please deliver this word to Mordecai," Esther said to Hathach. "Tell him that if I, or anyone for that matter, approach the king in the inner court without being summoned, I will be put to death. The only exception would be if the king extended his gold scepter. Only then would my life be spared."

As Hathach prepared to leave, Esther called after him, "Tell him also that it has been thirty days since I was called to the king."

Later

We waited for what seemed an interminable time. Finally Hathach returned. "I have delivered your message to Mordecai, Queen Esther, and I have returned with his reply. He has asked that I deliver the message in private."

Sohelia had already left to begin preparations for Esther's lunch. "It's all right, Hathach," Esther said. "Susiana will stay."

"As you wish," he said. "The following words are Mordecai's reply to you: 'Do not think that because you are in the king's house you alone of all the Jews will escape. For if you remain at this time, relief and deliverance for the Jews will arise from another place, but you and your father's family will perish. And who knows but that you have come to royal position for such a time as this?'"

Esther was silent, and then she turned to me and spoke so quietly I could barely hear her. "Haman knows. Mordecai is trying to tell me that Haman knows."

I didn't understand. I shook my head and looked at her confused. She leaned over and whispered in my ear. "Listen carefully to his words, 'Do not think you alone of all the Jews will escape.' Somehow he has found out that I am a Jew. Xerxes doesn't know or he wouldn't have ordered this, but Haman knows."

I thought immediately of Shaashgaz. He had overheard my conversation with Roxana. He was the one who told Haman. I remembered Sohelia's warning to me about the eunuchs.

Esther moved in her seat. "God help me," she whispered under her breath, and she turned to face Hathach. "Please deliver another message to Mordecai," she told him.

"Tell him to gather all the Jews in Susa and fast for me. Tell them not to eat or drink for three days and three nights. My maids and I will do the same. When this is done, I will go to the king, even though it is against the law. If I perish, I perish."

"Esther?" I pleaded. The Feast of Passover was to begin this night. It always began the evening before the fourteenth day of Nisan. I didn't know what to do.

She interrupted me. "I know what tomorrow is," she said. "You must be with your family. I want you to go. Eat as you normally would on this day. Your food tomorrow is not eaten for sustenance. It's symbolic. It represents the food the Jews ate when God set them free from their captors. We are captive now, and God will set us free, just as he set our ancestors free."

The Feast of Passover

Usually this is our time of celebration and great joy. At twilight Roxana and her parents and I gathered in Mother and Father's apartment. Every Jew in Susa had heard of the royal edict. We were all quiet, although I know our minds were anything but.

Father agreed with Esther. We would prepare our meal as God has directed us to. At all other times, we would fast.

So I jot these notes before we are to begin. I imagine it will be a Passover Feast like before; the table will be lit with little white candles, and we will sit around it, shoulder to shoulder. Father will give each of us a chunk of roasted lamb.

"This lamb," he will say quietly, "is a reminder of the sacrifice the Jews made just before they left Egypt. On a night just like this, they were gathered together in a hostile land. Each family sacrificed a lamb and smeared the blood on the doorposts and lintel."

Father's face will be silhouetted in the candlelight. I'll hear the story I've heard so many times, but perhaps it will seem more real to me this evening. If I close my eyes, will I too be in Egypt?

Surely I will hear Father continue as he always does. "Then they waited," he will say. Will I hear his voice quiver just a bit? "They held their breath and clung to their children while the angel of death crept by their doors, paused, and moved on. They listened to the screams of the Egyptians who cradled their dead children in their arms."

I imagine I will hear Roxana sigh and see her look away. She will be deep in thought. It will be difficult to not feel the gravity of our plight.

Why are we persecuted like this? What had we done then? What have we done now? This will be what Roxana is thinking. This is what I wonder even now as I think of the feast . . .

Yes, bitter herbs will be dished out to everyone. A salad of endive, dandelion, chicory, and sorrel will be eaten on the evening of the Passover. "These herbs, often bitter in taste," Father will say, "are a symbol of the bitterness of Israel's servitude to Egypt."

Then he will pass a bowl of unleavened bread around the table, and we will each take a piece. "This bread, made without yeast," Father will explain, "is the same bread our people took with them when they left Egypt. It's a reminder that they fled their captives in great haste in the dark of the night."

He will fill all of our cups with wine, and we will wait for the blessing. *"Barukhata Adonai Eloheinu Melekh ha'olam borei p'ree haeitz."* We will hear the traditional Hebrew blessing that means "Blessed are you Adonai our God, ruler of the universe, who creates the fruit of the tree." Then we will eat and we will drink.

We will sing songs of thanksgiving, and we

will say many prayers, more prayers than usual. I will sleep once again in my mother and father's apartment, and I will feel safe. Father always makes me feel safe.

I will tell him this as he wraps his arms around me before bedtime.

"My arms are just little, Susiana," he will say, as always. "There are bigger arms that can protect you much better than mine. Those belong to our God."

Surely, then I will sleep with peace.

It's Morning after the Feast

Mother woke me up with a cup of steaming tea. We sat with Father around the corsi. There was something I'd wanted to ask him since I'd arrived last evening.

"Father," I said, "Damaris was the one who originally told me the news. I was very surprised at how upset she was. She's not even a Jew. Then there was the eunuch Hathach—he was deeply disturbed too. I could see it in his eyes and hear it in his voice, by how he talked."

Father placed his hand over mine. "Susiana," he said, "the Jews have lived in Persia for some time now. We're not an island. Some have married Persians. Some are friends with Persians. Some, like us, work for Persians and have acquired Persian friends. If this deed is done, it will be carried out by men who have tasted blood. Once they taste the blood of a Jew, there will be no more distinction between the blood of a Jew or any other man."

I was confused. "Do you mean they'll kill Persians as well?" I asked.

Father nodded. "Of course," he said. "Do you think that if they walk into a home filled with people, that they'll stop to ask, 'Who among you is a Jew?' Do you think they'll take the time to kill a Jewish man but leave his Persian wife? Do you think they'll care that much? Do you think they'll be satisfied with the spoils of a Jew and leave the riches of the Persian? Who would know in the end? What authority would punish them?"

I nodded my head. I understood now. It wasn't just a crime against our people; it was a crime against mankind.

Esther Will Plead to Xerxes

It's early on the third day, and Esther has prepared herself to meet with King Xerxes. Sohelia and I waited in her bedchamber while Hathach chose her royal robes. It's a good thing that Esther didn't desire privacy today, because we all felt the need to stay close to her.

I am weak from hunger, and I know Esther must be too. Sohelia has even fasted to show her solidarity. Of course, she knows by now about Esther's heritage and her relationship to Mordecai. I secretly think she's known all along. She's too smart and far too observant.

The news of the edict has upset Sohelia very much. She cares deeply for Esther, and I know she's grown quite fond of me too. We've become like a family because we spend so much time together. I can read Sohelia's moods with surprising accuracy. She gives herself away with a flip of her head, the arch of a pointy gray eyebrow, or the way she holds her hands.

Esther had slipped behind a dressing screen earlier, and when she emerged I thought I would cry. Her caftan was made of rose-colored damask and embroidered with silver flowers. Her waist was cinched with a silver girdle inset with rows of the clearest diamonds. Her hair was even woven with diamonds and silver ribbon. She looked luminous, but her eyes betrayed her. I could see a hint of sadness and fear.

Sohelia painted Esther's lips and eyes and powdered her face and neck. She sprinkled perfume on her hair and stood back to admire the results. "You will return, you know," she told Esther. "You look far too beautiful to die today." This made Esther smile, but I frowned at Sohelia. Why did she have to mention that word?

Later

Hathach had taken great care to choose Esther's finery today. He knew he had to—if the queen wants to extract a favor from the king, it's considered wise to play up her beauty and her charms. The eunuchs are masters at this. Hegai had done the same when he dressed Esther to meet Xerxes for the first time.

This occasion was entirely different, however. Hathach rapped on the door and stepped in. He held out his arm for Esther, and she paused for a moment and looked at us.

I felt hot tears well up in my eyes, and I hoped they wouldn't overflow. I didn't want Esther to see them. I knew tears would upset her.

"The king sits upon his throne?" Sohelia asked Hathach.

"Yes," said Hathach, "and it would appear that he's in fairly good spirits today. Anything could change that, so I'd advise that we leave at once and do not risk anger with lateness."

Esther walked over to Sohelia and me. I could smell her sweetly perfumed hair. "Then I'll leave now," Esther announced, "but not without Sohelia and Susiana." My heart began to pound, and I saw Sohelia's eyebrows shoot up.

Hathach bowed his head in deference to Esther. "If it pleases the queen," he said demurely. He held the door wide, and with a sweep of his graceful arm, he ushered us past.

Sohelia motioned for me to carry the train of Esther's dress.

Each step to the king's hall felt like a thousand. I held the luxurious fabric in my fingers, and feared I would ruin it with the sweat of my hands. Sohelia's mouth was fixed in a tight line, though she would try to soften it and smile when Esther looked at her.

Esther walked with her head high and her shoulders squared, but I could hear her inhale deeply and slowly as if trying to calm her body and her mind. She wore a smile on her face, but I knew her heart was consumed with anguish.

We approached the outer court of the king's hall and slipped slowly and softly past the towering columns. Our leather boots, lifted with dread, were quiet on the marble floor, but we passed dozens of guards and counselors who stopped to stare at us as we walked by. Some sat on black marble benches; some stood.

Voices and deep-throated laughter drifted from the direction of the throne room. When we entered the inner court, there was a clear view to the king's hall. I suddenly saw King Xerxes seated on his throne and nearly gasped out loud.

His head was turned to the side as he listened to one of his cupbearers. He was seated on a tall, high-backed golden chair with a cushion. Its feet were shaped like lions' paws. Both of the king's feet rested on a footstool whose legs were made in the form of bulls' legs and hoofs. He held his gold scepter in his right hand. It was as long as he was tall, so the bottom of it rested on the floor.

Two robed guards stood behind Xerxes. I knew them to be members of the Persian army called the "ten thousand immortals." They stood at attention with their long spears resting on their toes.

On either side of the throne were two metal

incense burners. Frankincense burned inside them and swirled out of their tops in smoky plumes. An attendant stood near the burners with a metal pail filled with frankincense. His job was to refill the burners continuously so the incense never ran out.

A long, silk carpet lay between the throne and us. Then, as if in slow motion, Xerxes turned his head toward us. For the briefest second I thought I saw anger flash from his eyes. If it was there at all, it was gone in an instant, but it was too late. Esther had seen something too. I watched her sway in front of me and reach for Sohelia's arm. Sohelia tried her best to steady her and keep her on her feet, but Esther collapsed in a heap on the floor. She had fainted.

In an instant Xerxes leaped from his throne and rushed to Esther. He took her in his arms and laid the golden scepter upon her neck. Sohelia and I stood back, astonished. He helped her to her feet then and held out the scepter to her so she could touch its tip.

I could see that she still trembled, and

Xerxes asked her gently, "What is it, Queen Esther? What is your request? Even up to half the kingdom, it will be given you." His face was crumpled with concern for her. He seemed moved by Esther, and I was sure that he truly would've given her half the kingdom if only she'd asked.

Esther smiled at him. Her face was still pale, nearly translucent, but her eyes were alive. They beamed with gratitude toward Xerxes. "If it pleases the king," she replied, "let the king, together with Haman, come today to a banquet I have prepared for him."

"Bring Haman at once," the king announced to one of his eunuchs, "so that we may do what Esther asks."

We left the king's hall and returned to the harem to prepare for the banquet.

Esther sat limply on the divan. "It is by the grace of God that I am alive and well and have received such favor with the king," she whispered.

Sohelia ran off with Hathach to tend to the

details, and I sat at Esther's feet. "It is surely the grace of God," I agreed. "But, Esther, may I ask you a question?"

She nodded. "Of course. Anything."

"What prompted you to ask Xerxes and Haman to attend a banquet?" I had been puzzled by her request since I heard it. It was the very last thing I had expected to hear.

"I had to test Xerxes' devotion to me, Susi," she explained. "If he wasn't willing to attend a banquet I had prepared for him, he'd never tolerate my talking against Haman. He's his most trusted advisor."

"Secondly," she added, "if my theory is correct and Haman does know that I'm a Jew, he would undoubtedly be suspicious of my sudden appearance three days after the edict was announced.

"Who knows what further trouble he could stir up for me or for Mordecai or for our people in general? By holding a banquet and inviting Haman as well, maybe I have appeased him for a time."

I thought it was a very wise plan. I was impressed that Esther had thought it out so well. "So, as it stands now," I said, "Haman is most likely honored and flattered that you have included him in the king's banquet, and Xerxes thinks favorably of you for having done so."

"It would appear so," Esther agreed. "But, Susi," she told me, "remember one thing."

I will never forget. I will write Esther's words so no one can forget. "It's not my own doing," she said. "My steps are ordered by God. Just as he gave Aaron to Moses to speak his words, so he fills my mouth. I could never do this on my own. I believe it's as Mordecai said. I've come to royal position for such a time as this."

The First Banquet

King Xerxes and Haman attended the banquet Esther held for them. The king ate alone, as was the custom, but Haman and Esther were permitted to join him for wine. The cupbearers who had tested Xerxes' food earlier to make certain it was not poisoned now tasted his wine.

Sohelia and I hovered in the background, once again at Esther's request. It was apparent that Haman was delighted at the invitation. How could he not be? He was the only guest besides the king.

Xerxes lifted the silver cup to his lips and took a long, slow sip of the sweet wine. He never took his eyes off Esther. He set the cup down. "Now what is your petition?" he asked her. "It will be given you. And what is your request? Even up to half the kingdom, it will be granted."

Esther hesitated for a brief second and then spoke with confidence. "My petition and my request is this: If the king regards me with favor and if it pleases the king to grant my petition and fulfill my request, let the king and Haman come tomorrow to the banquet I will prepare for them. Then I will answer the king's question."

Xerxes agreed, and both he and Haman left.

"I don't like that Haman," Sohelia said

crossly. "Did you see the sly smile on his face? Even if I didn't know what I do know, I still wouldn't like him. There's something very wicked about him. He's not to be trusted."

Esther nodded. "I felt very strongly that the time was not right for me to talk to Xerxes about him. I can't explain it; I just knew I had to wait one more day."

When I went to bed this evening there was a note lying on my bed. It said, "Roxana wishes to meet with you tomorrow morning just past daybreak. She will wait for you in the laundry." It looked like Hathach's handwriting. I wonder how she got word to him.

It's Just after Daybreak

I crept out of the harem first thing this morning and found Roxana. I hugged her tightly and told her how I missed her.

"I've missed you too," she said. She smiled so sadly I thought my heart would break. "I hardly ever get to see you anymore, Susi."

"I know," I told her, "and I can't stay very long now." I pulled her into a corner of the laundry area behind tall stacks of neatly folded white towels. "Esther will meet with Xerxes and Haman one more time today."

"Yes, I know," she said.

I shook my head. "How could you possibly know?" I asked. "They were invited only yesterday, late in the afternoon."

"Damaris," Roxana said simply. "She found me last night. She has information for you, but she refuses to go back to the harem and deal with that guard—Samba, or whatever his name is. She asked if I could get word to you somehow."

"Oh no," I sighed and sank onto the floor. "Damaris rarely has good news."

Roxana sat down next to me. "I'm afraid you're right. It's not good. After Haman left the banquet yesterday, he passed Mordecai at the gate. Mordecai wouldn't even acknowledge him. Susi, Haman has ordered that a gallows be built so Mordecai can be hanged on it."

Roxana looked at me closely. "Listen carefully," she said. "He's going to visit the king this morning and ask that Mordecai be hanged on the gallows at once."

I felt my heart drop. I wished I could just sink through the hard, cold floor. Could things possibly get any worse?

I cried on Roxana's shoulder, like I cry as I write this. What can be done? The banquet isn't until this afternoon, and then it might be too late. I told Roxanna my fears. She wants me to go warn Esther. I wanted to think about it and thought, dear diary, you might somehow help me by showing me my thoughts in black and white. But now I see that I must just go. Things went so well yesterday. If only yesterday could be today . . .

Later

I arrived back in the harem, and the most unbelievable things happened. I heard several voices coming from Esther's bedchamber. One was deep, and I recognized it to be Hathach. I walked slowly up to the door and tried to hear what they were saying. "Yes," Hathach said, "Haman was already waiting in the outer court to speak to the king."

They must know already! I held my knuckles close to the door, ready to knock, when I heard Hathach again, "The king called for Haman and asked him, 'What should be done for the man the king delights to honor?' Naturally, Haman thought the king was referring to him!"

I couldn't just stand in the hallway and hear the terrible story told through a wooden door. I rapped on the doorpost, and Hathach opened it. "Oh, Susiana," Esther cried and pulled me into the room. "Hathach has brought us the most wonderful news!"

I stood there for a long moment. I had no idea what to say. Hathach and Esther and Sohelia stared at me. Finally, Esther took my hand in hers. "What is it?" she asked me. "Has something happened?"

"Well, yes," I said. "When I came back and knew that Hathach was here, I thought you knew. Now I'm very confused. You say you have wonderful news, but I've just heard the most horrible news."

A little smile lit the corners of her mouth then. "You've not heard then," she said. "Or rather you have heard, but only part of the story. There's much more to tell, and the story has the most wonderful ending. Sit down. Take heart. We'll explain."

I sat down and Esther and Hathach and Sohelia recounted the entire tale to me.

According to Hathach, late last night while Haman designed the gallows upon which to hang Mordecai, the king himself tossed and turned in his bed. When he realized that sleep would elude him, he called for his attendants. "Bring the book of the chronicles and read it to me," he told them. "Perhaps it will soothe my mind." The book of the chronicles is the history of Xerxes' reign.

The attendants carried in the papyrus scrolls,

pulled up several chairs, and took turns reading to the king. When they read the part about how Mordecai had exposed the plot by Bigthana and Teresh to assassinate the king, Xerxes held up his hand.

"What honor and recognition has Mordecai received for this?" he demanded.

"Well," they said, clearly puzzled, "it would appear that nothing has been done to honor him."

At that moment, Haman entered the outer court to speak to Xerxes about hanging Mordecai on the gallows. When the king's attendants told him that Haman waited to speak to him, he ordered that he be brought into his bedchamber.

"Haman," Xerxes said, "I would like very much to honor a man, but I need your suggestion on how to do it."

Haman, in his arrogance, assumed that Xerxes wanted to honor him. He told the king, "Dress him in one of the king's royal robes and bring him a horse that the king himself has ridden. Make sure this horse bears the royal crest on his head."

Xerxes listened and nodded while Haman spoke.

"Then," Haman continued after clearing his throat, "let the king's most noble princes lead him through the city on the horse. Let them proclaim, 'This is what is done for the man the king delights to honor!'"

"Splendid," the king cried. "Go at once. Get the robe and the horse and do just as you have suggested for Mordecai the Jew, who sits at the king's gate."

Haman stood there, frozen, as the king and his attendants looked on. "Go on," Xerxes urged. "Don't neglect anything you have recommended."

Sohelia clapped her hands after the story was told. "Isn't it just delicious?" she asked. I'd never seen Sohelia so animated.

"I can't believe it," I said. "It's the most wonderful news. The most amazing news."

"Yes," agreed Esther. "This very morning Haman will be leading Mordecai around the city."

"And the banquet?" I has asked Esther.

The banquet, she said, will be held shortly after they return.

The Second Banquet

Several hours ago, Esther came to find me. "Come Susi," she said, "it's time. Sohelia is waiting for us. The royal eunuchs have already summoned Haman."

I want to carefully record all that happened.

We were told that Haman had gone home immediately after the parade. He'd covered his head with ashes and mourned because he was so depressed. When he arrived at the banquet with the king, he didn't look remotely like the same man I'd seen the day before. Yesterday Haman had been jovial, and his eyes had sparked with arrogance. Today he was quiet and withdrawn; his eyes were vacant.

Once again, Esther and Haman joined the king for wine. They reclined on long, cushioned couches. Haman didn't participate in conversation unless a direct inquiry was made of him. He sulked, and more than once I noticed that Xerxes cast a disparaging glance in his direction.

Then, in the same manner as the day before, Xerxes picked up his silver cup and took a slow sip of his wine, never taking his eyes off of Esther. He put the goblet down. "Queen Esther," he said, "what is your petition? It will be given you. What is your request? Even up to half the kingdom, it will be granted."

Sohelia stood slightly in front of me, and I could see her squeeze her hands behind her back. The room was so still I could hear Esther take a breath before she began.

"If I have found favor with you, O king, and if it pleases your majesty," she said with calm confidence, "grant me my life—this is my petition. And spare my people—this is my request."

I watched Haman shift his body as if he couldn't find a comfortable place to rest. Xerxes' eyes clouded.

"For I and my people have been sold for destruction and slaughter and annihilation," she continued. "If we'd merely been sold as male and female slaves, I would have kept quiet, because no such distress would justify disturbing the king."

Xerxes slammed his fist upon the table. Haman jumped and tightened his grip on his silver chalice until his knuckles turned white. "Who is he?" the king roared. "Where is the man who has dared do such a thing?"

"The adversary and enemy is this vile Haman," Esther answered and turned to look in his direction.

Xerxes' face was red with rage. He abruptly left the hall and walked into the palace garden. Haman put his hand over his chest and began to gasp audibly. Esther was unmoved by Haman's theatrics, and she stayed on the couch and waited quietly.

"Why did Xerxes leave?" I whispered to Sohelia.

"He's very angry," Sohelia said. "I've seen him get angry on many occasions but never as angry as now. He probably wants to be alone and gather his wits about him."

Haman had moved closer to Esther, and he began to plead for mercy. "I know I have no chance with the king," he cried pitifully, "but you can change his mind. He'll listen to you."

He was on his knees before her when Xerxes returned from the garden. He stood and glared at him, a thousand daggers boring into his back. "What is this?" he cried. "Will he even molest the queen while she is with me in the house?"

At that moment, several eunuchs rushed forward and covered Haman's face with a veil. Haman stood still with his shoulders hunched. His arms hung limp at his sides. I saw Esther turn away and shudder visibly. Sohelia pulled me discreetly into a corner. "He has been condemned to die," she told me. "Persian kings refuse to look upon the face of a condemned man."

Then Harbona, another eunuch, stepped forward. "A gallows, seventy-five feet high stands by Haman's house," he told Xerxes. "He made it for Mordecai, who spoke up to help the king."

"Hang him on it!" Xerxes shouted. He was furious and stormed out of the hall.

Esther got up and stood close to us. She was pale, and her eyes looked weak. We watched the eunuchs lead Haman out of the room. She hugged Sohelia and kissed her gently on the cheek, and then she hugged me tight and kissed my cheek tenderly.

"It's never a happy day when a man is hanged," she said softly. "I wish it never had to come to this."

We walked slowly back to the harem, all of us deep in thought. Sohelia suddenly stopped and looked at both of us. "Haman will be dead by sunset," she said, "but the edict still lives." She said to Esther. "You know as well as I do that once a royal edict is proclaimed, it can't be reversed. Even Xerxes can't undo what has been done."

Esther shook her head. "It's not up to Xerxes," she said kindly. "It's up to God. What you saw take place today and what you heard take place last evening was all God's doing, not Xerxes' and certainly not mine. His marvelous hand has swept over this palace, and it will again and again and again."

Sohelia and I were silent. Then Sohelia said what I think Esther and I both had waited to hear from this woman we love, "I cannot deny that what I have seen so far is miraculous. If your God has truly done these things, then he truly is a great God.

The Gallows Are Haunting

Haman was hanged at sunset. He'd built the gallows seventy-five feet tall so when Mordecai was strung up, the entire city of Susa could witness his dishonorable death. Now he hangs from his own invention and Susa has looked upon him.

It is said that Xerxes' fury didn't subside until he knew that Haman had expelled his last breath.

A short while later, Harbona came to the

harem and summoned Esther. Sohelia and I stayed behind this time and are waiting for her to return. We have no idea what this is about, but Esther told us she wouldn't leave the king's presence until she'd pleaded for the lives of the Jews again.

Right after Esther left, I visited Mother and Father. I needed the comfort of them, to know they were safe. They were full of questions.

"Where is Mordecai now, Susi?" Mother asked me.

"He returned to the gate after the parade this morning, the same as always," I told her. "You know, Mother, it's funny. Esther said he never wanted any kind of reward for what he did. He was actually embarrassed. He reported the plot to Esther because it was the right thing to do. Haman, on the other hand, would do anything to be recognized by the king."

"Yes," Mother said, "and look at the out-come. God sees the hearts of all men, and he judges us accordingly. No one can hide."

Father had listened quietly until this. "It's

more than that," he interjected. "There are many, many unscrupulous leaders, but Haman tried to directly hurt our people. In our history, we have often been regarded as feeble, but God has proven time and again that we can be a formidable foe."

He was slicing open a pomegranate, and I watched the juice dribble onto the table. He gave Mother and me a slice.

"We don't seem like such a formidable foe now," I has said honestly.

Father looked at me, astonished. I will never forget his words then. "When Moses' back was pushed against the Red Sea and his face was turned toward the Egyptian army, he didn't seem so formidable, did he?" he said. "When Daniel was thrown into a lions' lair and stared into the mouths of a dozen hungry beasts, he didn't seem so formidable, did he?

"As Shadrach, Meshach, and Abednego were tossed into a blazing furnace so hot that it could melt their skin in less time than it takes for your heart to beat once, they didn't seem so formidable, did they?"

Father waited for me to answer.

"No," I admitted and hung my head. "They didn't."

"God will triumph in the midnight hour," he said. "If he triumphed a second sooner, we'd believe it was our doing and not his. It's written in our history. God has performed too many miracles through the ages for us to doubt him now, Susiana."

He was right. He always was. He'd rebuked me in a gentle way, and I was ashamed. But Mother and Father hugged me and the shame turned to gratefulness—for their faith and for God's mercy. He would take care of things as they should be if only I believed.

Esther Has Returned with Good News

The halls were dark and strangely quiet after I left Mother and Father and returned to see if Esther was back too. I never liked to walk those halls at night, and as I approached the harem, I heard a noise that made me whirl around.

What a relief it was to find it was Esther.

If I hadn't known her, I might have thought she was the beautiful ghost of the harem, for Esther was shrouded in shadows. Her long, black hair had been pulled loose from its braid, and her eyes shone luminously from the shadows. I want to record every detail of how she looked, what I heard and felt, and what happened then.

"Oh, Susi," she said in a whisper. "I've seen the power and the majesty of our Lord this evening." She stood there, almost floating in her long, pale robes.

I could only stand, staring, silent, in awe of her. She'd been transformed somehow and was more beautiful than I'd ever seen her.

"Esther! What happened?" I yelped and rushed to her side.

She took my hand.

"Come on," I said. "Let's go inside and you can tell me."

Sohelia stopped when she saw us. Her eyes were wide as she looked at Esther. She quickly led us into the courtyard and lit the torches. We sat on the garden benches and waited for Esther to talk to us. There was another full moon this evening. It illuminated the spindly trees and lit Esther's face.

"I arrived in the throne room tonight," Esther told us softly, "and Xerxes told me that Haman's estate has been given to me. Everything that Haman had is now mine. As you both know, that was the furthest thing from my mind."

Sohelia nodded her head rapidly. She was impatient to hear it all.

"Then I told Xerxes that Mordecai is my cousin," she said, "and he sent Harbona to summon him. When he arrived, Xerxes took off his large signet ring and gave it to Mordecai!"

I knew that Haman had originally been given the ring. It must've been pulled from his finger before he was hanged. The king's signet ring bears his royal crest on its gold face. Anyone who wears the ring has the authority to make decisions on the king's behalf. Xerxes had given Mordecai his royal signature!

I could scarcely believe this. "Esther," I cried. "Does this mean he holds the same position that Haman held? Is this possible?"

"Yes, yes!" she said. "It is possible, Susi. He's second only to the king! A purple robe was placed upon his shoulders, and a gold crown was set upon his head. He was given royal garments of blue and white!" A tear fell from her eye and slipped down her cheek. I don't think she was even aware of it.

Sohelia gasped. "I never thought I'd see as day such as this."

"It's only the beginning of what God has done," Esther said. "I promised you I would plead for the salvation of the Jews, and I did. I cried and fell at Xerxes' feet and begged him like a child would beg her father. He gave Mordecai and me the authority to write another decree in the king's name, on behalf of the Jews!"

Tears were falling swiftly now. "I haven't, in my lifetime, witnessed a miracle such as this," she said. "The decree gives the Jews the right to assemble and protect themselves on the thirteenth day of the month of Adar. Xerxes couldn't revoke his former decree, but he did make it possible for another to be written that can save the people. The people have the right to defend themselves against anyone who tries to harm them on that day."

I squeezed my eyes tight and tried not to cry. Sohelia's shoulders began to shake, and she held her face in her hands.

Tonight I think of this moment and realize the power of it: It had been the midnight hour, just as Father said, and God had rescued our people once again. It's not possible to look at the chain of events and believe that anyone but God was responsible for all the miracles of this day.

Then, I could see that Esther was still talking, but I couldn't hear what she was saying. My own thoughts were spinning—and spin still as I pen all of this now . . .

God had taken an unsuspecting little Jewish girl—an orphan, no less—and groomed her to become the Queen of Persia. If this is possible, is anything impossible with God?

Esther has saved her people, and that

includes me and Mother and Father and Roxana and her mother and father. Esther put aside her fears and risked her life to plead to the king on behalf of me and every Jewish boy and girl, every baby and mother and father, and every grandmother and grandfather in the entire Persian Empire!

Let Esther's story be told for years to come. If you read these words, you read my hope that her story is told to you just as the stories of Abraham, Moses, David, Daniel, and Shadrach, Meshach, and Abednego have been told to me.

Little boys and girls will climb up on their fathers' knees. "Father," they'll beg, "tell us the story of Esther, the brave queen who saved her people."

They'll say, just like I used to say to my father, "Is it true? Did this really happen?"

I can say now that it is true. It really did happen. I know because I was alive to see it all.

I watched Esther grow from a beautiful, kind girl to a compassionate, wise, and bold woman of faith. During that time, I had grown too. When I first entered the harem, I was terrified of the ghosts that lurked in the shadows. I have to admit, I'm still leery of the bathhouse, and I do look over my shoulder when I walk the halls at night.

Sometimes I think I see a pale wisp of robe slipping around the corner. Is it the ghost of the harem? Probably not, but I may always wonder. Esther has taught me to have confidence in God when the present is murky and frightening. Besides, Father was right all along. If God gives us a job to do, he has already equipped us with the means to do it.

I learned something else too. There's beauty in boldness. It's why Esther grew more beautiful every year. Her beauty didn't come from cosmetics and perfumes or from jewels and silk robes. The other girls never stood a chance. Esther's beauty came from within. It was a beauty that was born when she chose to honor God with her courage and with her faith.

It grew into a glowing radiance.

She truly is and always will be the star of Persia, reflecting the light of the one God, the true God of the heavens.

EPILOGUE

The months passed. Finally the dreaded thirteenth day of the month of Adar arrived. The palace of Xerxes was well guarded by the ten thousand immortals, the feared army of King Xerxes the Great. The Jews who lived within the palace walls, including Susiana, saw no attackers on that day.

The well-fortified city of Susa, however, was not so fortunate. Bloodthirsty men, armed with the king's original decree, stormed the gates, looking for Jews. They were stopped dead in their tracks. Not only were the Jews defended by spears, they were surrounded by the king's own nobles and officials. The Jews killed five hundred men that day, fighting for their lives and their posterity. They took nothing from their attackers. In all of the provinces, seventy-five thousand men died while attacking the Jews. The ten sons of Haman, who promised to avenge their father's death, were slain, hung on the high gallows like their father.

Mordecai rose to great prominence. He was

feared and respected in the whole of the Persian Empire to its most distant shores, and his reputation spread far and wide.

He and Queen Esther continued to toil on behalf of the Jews. They declared that a feast be celebrated every year to commemorate the victory of the Jews over the evil plot of Haman. They called it the Feast of Purim.

King Xerxes ruled the Persian Empire until 465 B.C., when he was found slain in his bedchamber. He was assassinated by his chief minister and one of his chief eunuchs. As a result, Queen Esther's miraculous thirteen-year reign came to an end that year. There was never a queen who was more loved by her people. It isn't known what became of her or Mordecai.

Sohelia, distressed after the assassination of Xerxes and the end of Esther's reign, left the palace at Susa and was never heard from again.

Roxana married and had two children. She continued her service at the palace and remained best friends with Susiana.

Damaris, on the other hand, never found a

suitable spouse. She stayed in the palace and remained a source of valuable information.

Two years after her last diary entry, Susiana married, much to her mother's relief. She and her husband, Abiel, had one child, a girl they called Hadassah. After Esther's reign ended, Susiana worked in the kitchen beside her mother. Years later, when her mother and father died, Susiana was promoted to chief pudding maker and Abiel became the master gardener.

Abiel lived to be eighty years old, and Susiana lived until she was almost ninety. When Hadassah sorted the belongings in her mother's trunk, she found a tiny package bound in a white handkerchief and tied with a silver ribbon. She pulled off the ribbon and examined the handkerchief. It was obviously very old, but it was still beautiful. Its thin edges were gently scalloped. In a corner, the name Hadassah was embroidered in yellow.

As she opened the bundle of paper and discovered her mother's diary, the dried petals of a once snow-white lily fluttered to her feet.

Cast of Characters...

Beautiful Esther

SUSIANA'S HOME

The story of Esther takes place in the Persian Empire between 479 and 474 b.c. Most of the action occurs in King Xerxes' winter palace in Susa, the Persian capital.

The People Susiana Wrote of Most

Esther: Jewish woman in royal harem and, later, queen of Persia

Herself: Esther's favorite, young, Jewish attendant *

Sohelia: Esther's older, experienced, Persian attendant *

Mordecai: Esther's Jewish cousin and an official at the palace

King Xerxes I: King of Persia

Haman: King Xerxes' closest personal advisor

Hathach: King Xerxes' royal eunuch, assigned to Queen Esther

Mother: Susiana's mom, a servant in the palace kitchens *

Father: Susiana's dad, a servant in the palace garden *

The People Susiana Encountered

(in order of appearance)

Roxana: Susiana's best friend, also Jewish *

Damaris: Persian palace servant and gossip *

Hegai: Royal eunuch in charge of harem

Ava: Palace servant *

Biztha: Royal eunuch *

Moj: Girl in harem *

Leyla: Girl in harem *

Zeynah: Girl in harem *

Sumbul: Harem guard *

Bundle woman: Jewish merchant *

Harbona: Royal eunuch

Bigthana and Teresh: Two of the king's eunuchs

* Fictional characters

King Xerxes,
as he tries on one of his
many fine robes.

His portrait can be found on
many of the coins we use to
buy things.

Haman hated Mordecai, and wanted to get rid of all the Jews in Persia.

Mordecai, in shock at the new decree.

Artifacts . . .

Lots similar to this one may have been used by Haman to fix the date for the destruction of the Jews in Persia.

Ornate decorations like this lions head were worn on garments.

Many fine cups like this one adorned the King's dining h

Art and Writing...

The palace is full of beautiful sculptures and carved pillars.

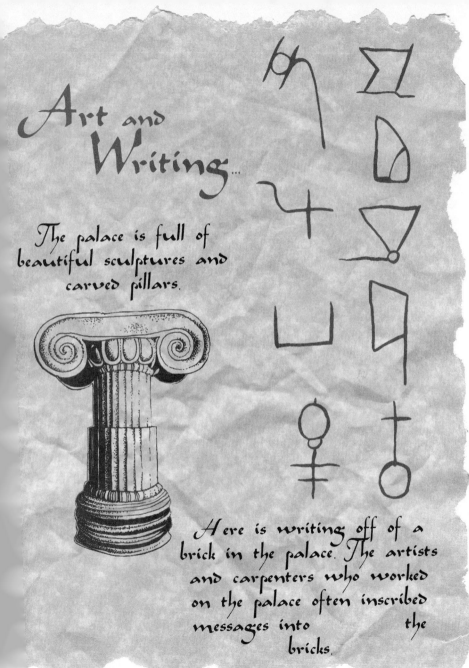

Here is writing off of a brick in the palace. The artists and carpenters who worked on the palace often inscribed messages into the bricks.

TRACING HISTORY: A TIMELINE

587 B.C.

Babylon, under the leadership of King Nebuchadnezzar, invades Jerusalem and plunders God's holy temple. The city and temple are torched. Several thousand of the brightest Jews are rounded up and taken to Babylon, where they will live in exile.

539 B.C.

The Babylonian Empire falls to the Persians.

537 B.C.

Cyrus the Great, first king of the Persian Empire, issues a decree that allows the Jewish exiles to return to Jerusalem. Many do, and a small group of them begin to rebuild the temple. Many others do not. They have lived and worked in Persia for many years, and Cyrus allows them the freedom to practice their own religion.

520 B.C.

Darius the Mede is crowned king of Persia.

486 B.C.

Darius dies and his son, Xerxes, ascends the throne.

483 B.C.

King Xerxes holds a banquet prior to his invasion of Greece. He calls for his wife, Queen Vashti, to appear before his guests. She refuses, and Xerxes divorces her for her blatant disobedience.

479 B.C.

The search begins for a new queen. Young, never-married women are summoned to the king's harem in the palace of Susa. Esther, beautiful and Jewish, is one of those women. She is cousin to Mordecai, an official at the palace. The women undergo one year of beauty and purification treatments.

478 B.C.

Esther is summoned to the king and proclaimed queen.

474 B.C.

Xerxes promotes Haman to the position of vizier. He is the king's closest advisor.

Mordecai refuses to prostrate before him, so Haman plots to have him destroyed.

Haman convinces Xerxes to issue a decree to kill all Jews in the Persian Empire on the thirteenth day of the Jewish month of Adar.

Esther goes before the king unannounced. She pleads on behalf of her people and reveals her Jewish heritage to Xerxes for the first time.

Haman is hanged on the gallows. Mordecai is promoted to his position. A new decree is drafted that allows all Jews to defend themselves.

473 B.C.
In self-defense, Jews throughout the Persian Empire kill 75,000 of their attackers.

The Feast of Purim, which celebrates the Jews victory over Haman's deadly plot, is celebrated for the first time.

465 B.C.
King Xerxes is murdered. His son, Artaxerxes I, becomes the new king of Persia.

A map of the
Persian Empire

Black Sea

Caspian Sea

Persian Empire

The Great Sea
(Mediteranean Sea)

Assyria

Parthia

Libya

Judea

○ Susa
Setting of the book of Esther

Egypt

Persian Gulf

Arabia

Red Sea

Erythraean Sea

PERSIA'S PLACE IN HISTORY

Cyrus, the first king of the Persian Empire, was the only Gentile king ever to be anointed by God. One hundred and fifty years before Cyrus ruled Persia, the prophet Isaiah spoke of him:

> This is what the Lord says to his anointed, to Cyrus, whose right hand I take hold of to subdue nations before him and to strip kings of their armor, to open doors before him so that gates will not be shut: I will go before you and will level the mountains; I will break down gates of bronze and cut through bars of iron. I will give you the treasures of darkness, riches stored in secret places, so that you may know that I am the Lord, the God of Israel, who summoned you by name.
>
> For the sake of Jacob my servant, of Israel my chosen, I summon you by name and bestow on you a title of honor, though you do not acknowledge me.
>
> Isaiah 45:1-4

> I will raise up Cyrus in my righteousness: I will make all his ways straight. He will rebuild my city and set my exiles free, but not for a price or reward, says the Lord Almighty.
>
> Isaiah 45:13

In October 539 B.C., Cyrus invaded Babylon, and King Belshazzar could not hold off the Persian forces. Belshazzar's mighty city, besieged unexpectedly during the night, folded like a paper fan. Just as Isaiah prophesied, the Persian army found all of Babylon's gates wide open. One hundred massive brass gates, twenty-five on each of the four sides of the city, swung open on their hinges, their iron bars mysteriously unlocked. The gates of the palace swung open as well, as if to welcome the invaders into their midst.

Every part of the city, normally shut tight at dusk, was open to the Persian soldiers. Those who lived in the outskirts of Babylon were taken prisoner well before an alarm ever reached the center of the palace.

Discovered in the underground vaults were the "treasures of darkness and riches stored in secret places" that God had promised Cyrus (Isaiah 45:3). Thirty-four thousand pounds of gold, and five hundred thousand talents of silver, in addition to golden vases and other priceless treasures, were found. Not long after, Cyrus ended the Jews' exile in Babylon, where they had been held captive for seventy years. He made a proclamation throughout his empire and put the following words on paper, a promise for all time:

> The Lord, the God of heaven, has given me all the kingdoms of the earth and He has appointed me to build a Temple for Him at Jerusalem in Judah. Anyone of his people among you—may his God be with him, and let him go up to Jerusalem in Judah and build The Temple of the Lord, the God of Israel, the God who is in Jerusalem.
>
> Ezra 1:1–3

More than 40,000 Jews left Babylon and returned to Palestine. Cyrus not only pledged his "blessing" in the rebuilding of the temple, but also offered his financial support. He demanded nothing in return.

Cyrus is the author of the first Charter of Human Rights known to mankind. He considered himself a liberator rather than a conqueror, and he proved it by extending social and religious tolerance toward his newly acquired kingdoms. Immediately after he conquered Babylon, he addressed the people in their own language. It was an unheard of display of respect, and insured for history books that his benevolence toward his subjects would be well-known.

At its height, the Persian Empire stretched from India to Greece and from the Caspian Sea to the Red Sea and the Arabian Sea.

King Cambysses, son of Cyrus, is credited for conquering Egypt. King Darius is recognized for his organization of the kingdom, for partially defeating the Greeks, for organizing the first postal system, and for designing and building the palaces at Persipolis and Susa. King Xerses continued the war against the Greeks and the construction of the two palaces.

Two centuries later, the Persian Empire met Alexander the Great—and its demise. Under Alexander's rule, the Greeks would hold the land and the Jewish people in an iron grip. But that is another story . . .

**Stay tuned for more
Promised Land Diaries**

THEN AND NOW

The city of Susa is one of the oldest cities in the world. Persian tradition even says it's the first city in the world. It was built by King Hushang, the same man who discovered how to make fire using steel and flint. Over the course of four thousand years, thirteen cities were built, one upon the other. Archaeologists uncovered fragments that show that at least fifteen different languages were used in the city of Susa throughout its long history.

In 530 B.C. Cyrus the Great made Susa the capital of Persia. It was the ideal city for this purpose because it rested in the middle of his empire. It also lay on the fertile banks of the Choaspes River, famous for its pure, flowing water.

It is said that King Cyrus would drink only the water from the Choaspes. If he left the area, he sent his servants to the river to draw the pure water and store it in silver vessels. Four-wheeled wagons pulled by mules carried the vessels and followed the king wherever he went.

The king spent winters in Susa and springtime in Persipolis, his ceremonial capital to the south. In the summer months, he traveled further north to the cool mountains of Ecbatana.

When Darius I succeeded Cyrus, he built an impressive palace in Susa on a raised platform measuring 820 feet by 490 feet. Fine cedar wood was brought down from Lebanon. Egyptian artisans crafted the gold, ivory, silver, ebony, lapis lazuli, and turquoise. Skilled Babylonian artisans designed bricks and painted them in glazes of blue, green, white, and yellow.

The great central hall was 343 feet long and 244 feet wide. The king's gate, where Mordecai sat, is thought to have been a hall about 100 feet square. It's believed that the inner court where Esther appeared before King Xerxes was located between these two halls.

A high wall was built around the entire palace platform, and watchtowers projected high into the sky. A deep moat of mirky water snaked around the perimeter of the palace.

Today, little remains of the legendary city that once controlled important trade routes from ancient Mesopotamia eastward through the Zagros Mountains. Its ruins lie in the province of Khuzestan in southwest Iran.

BIBLIOGRAPHY

Many sources were consulted and used in research for writing Susiana's and Esther's story in the Promised Land Diary series, including:

Adam Clarke's Commentary on the Bible, Adam Clarke, abridged by Ralph H. Earle (World Bible Publishing Co., 1996).

The Golden Age of Persia: History of Civilization, Richard N. Frye (Phoenix Press, a division of The Orion Publishing Group Ltd., 1975 and 2000 paperback edition).

Ancient Persia, Josef Wiesehofer, and translated by Azizeh Azodi (I.B. Tauris Publishers, 1996 and 2001 paperback edition).

Atlas of the Bible: An Illustrated Guide to the Holy Land, editor Joseph L. Gardner (The Readers Digest Association, 1981).

The Atlas of Mysterious Places, consulting editor Jennifer Westwood (Barnes and Noble edition, 1998).

Biblical Literacy: The Most Important People, Events, and Ideas of the Hebrew Bible, Rabbi Joseph Telushkin (William Morrow and Company, 1997).

Essential Judaism: A Complete Guide to Beliefs, Customs, and Rituals, George Robinson (Pocket Books, a division of Simon & Schuster, 2000).

Harem: The World Behind the Veil, Alev Lytle Croutier (Abbeville Press Publishers, 1989, first paperback edition).

History of the Persian Empire, A. T. Olmstead, author (The University of Chicago Press, 1948 and 1959 paperback edition).

Jamieson, Fausset, and Brown's Commentary on the Whole Bible, Fausset, Brown, and Robert Jamieson (Zondervan, 1999).

Matthew Henry's Commentary on the Whole Bible: Complete and Unabridged in One Volume, Matthew Henry (Hendrickson Publishers, 1991).

Meredith's Book of Bible Lists, J. L. Meredith (Bethany House Publishers, 1980).

The New International Dictionary of the Bible, revising editor J.D. Douglas and general editor Merrill C. Tenney (Zondervan Publishing House, 1987).

Persia and the West, John Boardman (Thames & Hudson, 2000).

Women in Ancient Persia: 559–331 B.C., Maria Brosius (Oxford University Press, 1996 and 1998 paperback edition).

Women of the Bible: A One-Year Devotional Study of Women in Scripture, Ann Spangler & Jean E. Syswerda (Zondervan, 1999).

ABOUT THE AUTHOR

Anne Tyra Adams is the author of eight children's books, several of which have been translated into three foreign languages: Indonesian, Korean, and Afrikaans. Two of her books, *The New Kids Book of Bible Facts* and *The Baker Book of Bible Travels for Kids*, provided the foundation for writing this series, the Promised Land Diaries.

A journalist and detailed researcher, Adams is also a "student of ancient history," with a deep fascination for the Jewish culture. She used all this experience, love of history, and curiosity to write this book.

When not working on more Promised Land Diaries, Adams loves to read the classics and ancient history, taking many armchair travels in time to foreign lands. She especially loves reading biographies of famous authors.

She and her husband and their two children live in Phoenix, Arizona. They often hike in the mountainous desert surrounding their home and have been known to spot quail, coyote, an occasional fox, and many lizards. Not to be outdone by the great outdoors, they share their home with three dogs, a cat, and an assortment of little fish.

ABOUT THE ILLUSTRATOR

Dennis Edwards is the illustrator of three big Bible story-books: *Heroes of the Bible, Boys Life Adventures,* and *My Bible Journey.* As a designer and illustrator he's also contributed to numerous others.

His favorite books include Robert Louis Stevenson's *Treasure Island*, comic books, and science fiction-related books because "the sky's the limit!"

Dennis also enjoys acting, and at times gets to perform for the kids at his church.

Books in

Series
1
Persia's Brightest Star
The Diary of Queen Esther's Attendant

2
The Laughing Princess of the Desert
The Diary of Sarah's Traveling Companion

For my father, Joseph Russo,
who inspired me to read and learn.

For my mother, Theresa Russo,
who inspired me to write and use
my imagination.

For Mike and for my children—
Michal and Alexandra

© 2003 by Baker Book House

Published by Baker Books
a division of Baker Book House Company
P.O. Box 6287, Grand Rapids, MI 49516-6287
www.bakerbooks.com

Printed in the United States of America

Library of Congress Cataloging-in-Publication Data is on file at the Library of Congress,
Washington D. C.

Adams, Anne
ISBN 0-8010-4518-5

Scripture is taken from the HOLY BIBLE, NEW INTERNATIONAL VERSION®. NIV®. Copyright ©
1973, 1978, 1984 by International Bible Society. Used by permission of Zondervan. All rights reserved.

Series Creator: Educational Publishing Concepts, Anne Adams Tyra
Designer/Illustrator: Dennis Edwards
Editors: Jeanette Thomason, Kelley Meyne

The biblical account of Queen Esther can be found in the Bible's Old Testament. While Susiana's
diaries and the epilogue are based on this and historical accounts, the character of Susiana, her diaries,
and some of the minor events described are works of fiction.